For the briefest of moments, Lindsey wondered what it would be like to let Matt Alessandro under her skin— into her life and into her heart.

He leaned toward her and she held her breath, releasing it sharply when the tea kettle squealed.

Suddenly, reality scattered her idiotic thoughts as she shut off the burner. Matt Alessandro's father was responsible for her mother's murder, her father's depression and death, and her shattered life. And here she stood, inches away from touching his son. Kissing his son. Or worse. What in the hell was wrong with her?

"Do you want me to stay with you tonight?" Matt asked.

Did she? "No." Lindsey stepped away then. "I'll be fine."

"What if you get another threatening call?"

"I'll call you." She caught herself. "Or I'll call my uncle."

Suddenly she needed Matt out of her house, before her resolve crumbled. "You know, I'm exhausted suddenly...."

"Okay, I'll go. Remember to lock up."

"Always," Lindsey said, relieved when he stepped outside and shut the door behind him.

But just as Matt's taillights disappeared, the phone rang....

KATHLEEN LONG

WHEN A STRANGER CALLS

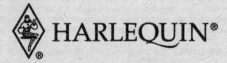

TORONTO • NEW YORK • LONDON
AMSTERDAM • PARIS • SYDNEY • HAMBURG
STOCKHOLM • ATHENS • TOKYO • MILAN • MADRID
PRAGUE • WARSAW • BUDAPEST • AUCKLAND

For Mom,
the most important heroine in my life.
I love you.

ISBN 0-373-22914-3

WHEN A STRANGER CALLS

ABOUT THE AUTHOR

After a career spent spinning words for clients ranging from corporate CEOs to talking fruits and vegetables, Kathleen Long now finds great joy spinning a world of fictional characters, places and plots. She shares her life with her husband and their neurotic Sheltie, dividing her time between suburban Philadelphia and the New Jersey seashore, where she can often be found—hands on keyboard, bare toes in the sand—spinning tales. After all, life doesn't get much better than that.

Please visit www.kathleenlong.com for the latest contests, appearances and upcoming releases.

Books by Kathleen Long

HARLEQUIN INTRIGUE
847—SILENT WARNING
914—WHEN A STRANGER CALLS

CAST OF CHARACTERS

Lindsey Tarlington—Daughter of Camille Tarlington and partner in Polaris, an agency dedicated to uncovering facts. When her mother's long lost identification appears, she begins an investigation into the past.

Matt Alessandro—Public defender and son of Tony Alessandro. He's vowed to prove his father's innocence and clear the family name. He convinces Lindsey to help him reopen her mother's case.

Frank Bell—Mayor of Haddontowne and Lindsey's uncle. He's on the fast track for the governor's mansion and doesn't want Matt revisiting the case that made his career.

Priscilla Bell—Mentally unstable and a recluse, she's Camille Tarlington's surviving sister and Lindsey's aunt. Does she know something about the night Camille vanished?

Doug Tarlington—Lindsey's father. He died in a suspicious one-car accident several years after Camille's disappearance. Was his death the result of a broken heart...or did he know the truth behind Camille's murder?

Lorraine Mickle—A former employee at Tony Alessandro's flower shop. She was the star witness for the prosecution of Matt's father, but was she telling the truth then? How about now?

Jimmy Freeman—A local handyman. He appears in Lindsey's neighborhood at the same time Camille's personal belongings begin to appear. Does he have a connection to the case?

Camille Tarlington—Lindsey's mother. She disappeared seventeen years earlier after an alleged lover's quarrel with Matt's father. Was her murder the result of an affair gone wrong? Or was the motive something altogether different?

Tony Alessandro—Matt's father. Prosecuted for the murder of Camille Tarlington, he died in jail six months later. Did he die an innocent man? Or was he guilty all along?

Chapter One

Raindrops slapped the small glass panes of the bedroom's French doors, and lightning illuminated the room, splashing against the plaster walls like an unexpected searchlight.

Lindsey Tarlington pulled the quilt up over her ears, her heart dancing against her ribs. The move was a futile attempt to block the inevitable thunder—the thunder she'd hated for the past seventeen years. Irrationally. Childlike.

The loud rumbling followed. A series of booming, rolling explosions that set her teeth on edge. The storm was moving closer. Too close for her liking.

She rolled over onto her back and tossed off the quilt, staring up at the lazy rotation of the rattan ceiling fan. The smell of damp, spring rain eased around the windows and doors, finding its way into the old house.

Another flash. Lindsey squeezed her eyes shut but then snapped them open. She was twenty-nine years old. It was long past time to get over her fear of storms.

Thunder crashed again, and she fisted the sheet tightly in both hands. Longer. The time between the flash and the boom had taken longer. Perhaps the core of the storm would miss her—miss the house she'd lived in all her life.

Another bang sounded and she narrowed her eyes at the ceiling. A car door?

Moments later, a familiar squeak filled her mind's eye with the image of the screen door hinge she kept forgetting to oil. A sliver of fear shimmied down her spine, and her breath caught. Who could be at her front door in the middle of the night? In the middle of a raging storm?

Lindsey tossed off the covers and moved to the French doors, trying to peer over the balcony. Rain sheeted the old, thick glass, but even so, she could make out the silhouette of a car, its headlights slashing through the storm as it idled out front.

Flashes of another night seventeen years earlier played through her mind. It had been a storm just like this one. There had been a steady stream of people in and out of the same screen door that night. Family. Friends. Police.

The sounds of running footsteps jarred her from the unwanted memories, but the rain had intensified, obscuring her view. A door slammed and the headlights eased away from the curb.

What if someone had left information on one of her cases?

Lindsey plucked her robe from the back of the rocker

and shrugged it on as she headed for the hallway, the wide pine planks cool and reassuring beneath her feet.

She stopped a few steps from the bottom of the staircase. No light glowed through the leaded windows on either side of the front door and her pulse kicked up a notch. Hadn't she just changed that bulb?

A low, anxious trembling hummed to life in her belly, and she concentrated for a moment. Concentrated on controlling the irrational fear—the quickening breaths.

She drew air in through her nose, holding her breath for several beats then releasing it slowly through tense lips.

"Get a grip, Tarlington."

Lightning flashed again as she reached for the doorknob. Thunder crashed at the precise moment she snapped open the inner door. She started, adrenaline zinging through her body.

Lord, she hated storms.

A second flash of lightning caught the small, white envelope tucked inside the storm door. She knelt quickly, pulling it free before it got soaking wet.

She slipped a finger beneath the flap as she turned, pushing the wooden door closed with her backside, glad to have its heavy thickness between her and the elements.

A single sheet of paper lay folded inside. Lindsey reached for the hall light switch, flipping it on with one hand as she shook open the sheet of paper with the other.

Her focus dropped instantly to the face centered on

the paper. A face she hadn't seen in seventeen years and thought she'd never see again.

Sudden panic filled her. She sank to her knees, her gaze riveted to the photocopy.

The police had never found a purse—had never found personal effects. No clothing. No jewelry. No identification. Yet here Lindsey sat, staring into the face on a photocopied driver's license. The driver's license that had gone missing seventeen years before on a stormy night just like this one.

Tears welled in her eyes as the pain, the shock, the unfairness of it all came rushing back. The familiar crush of grief wrapped its fingers around her heart and squeezed.

She stared into the photocopy of her mother's face and let the tears fall. Blood evidence found in her mother's abandoned car and at the floral shop where she'd worked had been enough to prove her death and convict her killer. Unfortunately, the clues hadn't been enough to locate her mother's body, still missing after all these years.

She'd never doubted her mother had been murdered, but she'd always feared the horror of her mother's final moments might resurface someday.

Lindsey dropped the paper and hugged herself.

It appeared someday had just arrived.

MATT ALESSANDRO STARED AT the sign anchored to the cinder block wall. Polaris Group. He remembered reading a newspaper article that had spelled out the history behind the organization. The group of friends had all experienced some sort of loss in their lives. Each had vowed to help others in similar situations find the truth—whatever that might be.

He'd read news of Lindsey Tarlington's work countless times, but the thought of seeing her in person had kicked his state of alert to a frenzy. He usually experienced this sort of hyperawareness during the first day of court, not at the mere thought of meeting someone.

Of course, it wasn't every day you met the daughter of the woman your father had been convicted of murdering. Falsely convicted—but convicted just the same.

Old bitterness welled from deep inside Matt's gut. He swallowed it down, straightening as he jerked open the entry door.

A petite blonde sat just inside, her desk facing the door. "Can I help you?"

Matt's lips curved into a warm smile, the move belying the cold determination he felt inside. "Lindsey Tarlington, please." He forced his voice past the sudden tightness in his throat. He had to handle this visit carefully. Lindsey Tarlington might very well be the key to what had really happened all those years ago. He hadn't been able to turn up any additional information, hadn't uncovered a single new clue, not until her late night delivery.

The blonde frowned, obviously picking up on his hesitation. "Is she expecting you?"

Matt shook his head. "No. This will only take a minute." Truth was, he hoped it would take far longer.

He hoped what he'd come to say would pique Lindsey Tarlington's interest enough to talk. Perhaps enough to share information.

Word of the photocopied license had buzzed quickly from the local police precinct to the public defender's office. After all, everyone knew he'd vowed to clear his dad's name—even after his old man had been killed on the inside.

His father might never have the chance to be set free, but his name did. Matt had dreamed of little else since his sixteenth birthday. The day they'd buried his father.

"May I tell her what it's about? She's on the phone." The blonde's pale brows arched, her green eyes widening.

Matt flashed his ID so fast she'd never be able to catch his name. "I'm with the Public Defender's office. It's in reference to a client of mine." A half-truth…sort of. "I thought she might be interested in the case."

Her expression morphed from suspicious to interested in the blink of an eye.

"Why don't you have a seat over there." She jerked her thumb toward the corner cubicle and a row of uncomfortable-looking chairs. "You can wait outside her door."

Matt glanced in the direction she'd indicated. The space consisted of three cubicles bordering a small central area. Pale grays and pinks adorned the walls and carpeting, no doubt chosen to soothe agency clients searching for answers, loved ones, closure. Simplistic artwork graced the outside of each cubicle.

Apparently the tenants were more focused on their work than on presenting a stylish image. He had to give them credit for that. He crossed the open area in four strides, stopping short when his gaze landed on the woman inside the corner office.

A lot had changed in seventeen years.

Her father may have kept her out of the courtroom, but Matt remembered the newspaper articles and the photos. Back then, Lindsey Tarlington had been a striking child.

She'd become a breathtaking woman.

Long, black hair draped loosely around her slender shoulders, falling like a waterfall of night sky. Her profile hinted at strong features, an aristocratic nose and full lips.

She sat perpendicular to him, her gaze focused on an open folder and a stack of photos. She fingered one as she talked. When she crossed her legs, several inches of creamy, smooth thigh peeked from beneath the hem of her black skirt.

Matt swallowed, more than enjoying the view. Heat warmed his neck, and he reached to loosen his tie, but caught himself, lowering his hand to his side. When Lindsey's slender fingers tugged at the hem of her skirt, he lifted his gaze to hers.

Ice-blue daggers made it clear his appreciation hadn't been welcomed. She hung up the phone and stood. Tall. Slender. Mesmerizing.

"Was there something I could help you with?"

Her palpable annoyance snapped Matt's attention

from his inappropriate focus on Lindsey Tarlington, the woman, to Lindsey Tarlington, the daughter.

"I'm Matt Alessandro. Tony's son."

With just those few words, all color drained from her cheeks. She sank back onto her chair. "Did you send me the copy?"

"No." Matt entered the cubicle, stepping so close he could feel her body heat as she stared up at him, wide-eyed. "But I'd like to help you find out who did."

THE MAN MAY AS WELL have sucked the air out of Lindsey's lungs.

He bore a shocking resemblance to his father—the unkempt mahogany hair, the clean-shaven, angular jaw, the hazel eyes more brown than green.

She blinked, willing him to disappear like an unwanted apparition, but he remained. In the flesh. In her office.

"You have no business here." Anxious trembling built inside her. She fought to remain still, to hide the raw emotion that had threatened to smother her since her discovery the night before.

"My father didn't kill your mother."

His words reignited the familiar, aching loss. Memories assailed her. News vans covering every inch of the curb in front of her home. Reporters stalking her at school. Her father shoving her onto a plane to stay with family far away.

Her mother. Missing. Vanished as if she'd never existed at all.

Emotion welled in Lindsey's throat. She had to get Alessandro's son out of her office—out of her sight. "Please leave. I've turned the matter over to the police."

He stood his ground, unflinching. Determination flashed in his piercing glare, as if he saw right through her brave facade. "Don't you make a living helping people discover the truth?"

Lindsey's gaze locked with his. Two could play this game. "I do. But my services aren't needed in a case like this. We already *know* the truth."

A shadow passed across Matt Alessandro's face. A flicker of sympathy teased at her heart, but she shoved it away. He might have lost his father, but murderers deserved whatever they got—and his father had been a cold-blooded killer.

He stepped closer, now seriously invading her personal space. She pushed the chair back with her knees and stood, surprised to discover he stood a full half head taller than her five feet eight inches.

"I find it difficult to believe someone with your reputation for sniffing out the facts would believe your late-night delivery means nothing."

Lindsey shrugged, hoping the move belied the doubt simmering in her gut. "Maybe it's someone's sick idea of a joke. Maybe someone who knew your father in jail decided to drop off one of his souvenirs."

Matt winced, but quickly recovered, a muscle twitching in his jaw.

She continued. "The police are all the help I need in the matter, Mr. Alessandro. Thanks for stopping by."

She turned her back, concentrating on shuffling the folders on her credenza.

"Then I'd like to hire your firm."

Lindsey breathed in sharply. The man could not take a hint. She turned on her heel, leveling a look that had chased off many unwanted clients—and men—before him. "I'm not interested in your business. Thank you."

Her clipped tone wavered, and she mentally berated herself. She had no desire to let the man see he'd rattled her.

Alessandro pulled a business card from the inside pocket of his tweed sport coat. He pressed the card to her desk, not allowing her the option of refusing.

"When you're ready to talk, give me a call. I'm sure you're intelligent enough to question who sent you that copy. I'm also sure deep down you question the convenience of my father's stabbing."

His intense stare bore through every defensive wall she'd erected. Lindsey flattened one hand against the back of her chair to steady herself.

"The real killer's still out there, Ms. Tarlington. I'd think you'd be more than a little concerned about that."

She stood her ground as he spun on his heel, crossed the small office, and pushed open the exit door. When he had safely gone, she conceded to the trembling in her knees, sinking onto the worn leather seat of her chair.

Lindsey tentatively touched the edge of his card, dragging it to the center of her desk.

Matt Alessandro.

She squeezed her eyes shut and rubbed a hand across her weary face. As if the copy of her mother's identification hadn't been enough, now the killer's son had reached out.

She gathered the case files from the desktop and shoved them into her briefcase. She plucked Alessandro's card from where it lay then dropped it into her trash can.

Snapping off her desk lamp, she steeled herself, wanting nothing to do with the man's soapy scent still lingering in her small cubicle.

"Patty." Lindsey paused at the office manager's desk as she headed toward the door. "I'm going out. You can reach me on my cell if anyone needs me."

Lindsey cast a glance toward her two partners, heads bent low over their own case files, working the phones. She should be doing the same, but right now she needed to put space between herself, Matt Alessandro's visit and her memories. The more space, the better.

She pushed out into the fresh, spring air, shoving the lingering guilt from her mind.

Ten minutes later she turned her car onto the tree-lined street, sighing with relief as her family home eased into view. The cherry blossoms displayed their full blooms, and the heavy buds on her favorite, old dogwood hinted at additional flowering beauty to come.

Lindsey breathed deeply of the sweet air filtering through her lowered car window. Spring in South Jersey. This had been her favorite time of year as a child, but on that April night years before, her world had tilted on its axis and never quite righted itself. In time, she'd learned to welcome the warmer days, but she never got over the irrational dread that accompanied the change of season each year.

A lone figure walked down her center sidewalk and away from the house as she eased her Volkswagen into the drive. Lindsey's stomach tightened. She slammed the car into Park and scrambled from her driver's seat. "Can I help you?"

Her voice rang out surely, in direct opposition to the rapid beating of her heart. What was he doing? Could it be the man who'd left the envelope?

The figure tensed then waved, keeping his head low as he turned away from her. Close-cropped silver hair hugged the lower half of his skull, as if his baldness hadn't quite yet won the battle. His shoulders remained hunched, the result of either years of poor posture or the ravages of time.

Loose papers fluttered in his hand as he continued down the block, turning up the next-door neighbor's front walk.

A harmless, elderly man passing out flyers.

Embarrassment and relief flooded through Lindsey. She couldn't take any more excitement today. Thank goodness her case count was low right now. The agency had been hired to find a few birth parents and one long-lost heir. Nothing more. Surely she could clear her head enough to manage that.

She plucked her briefcase from the floor behind her seat then slammed the car door. A sheet of paper sat tucked in the screen door handle, catching her eye as she crossed the front yard. She yanked it free, letting her gaze drop to the simple wording touting affordable lawn care. Glancing around at her overgrown garden and shrubs, she could understand why he'd picked her house.

She folded the flyer in half and slipped it into her briefcase. Professional help wasn't such a bad idea, actually. Her mother had always loved working in the garden. Somehow, Lindsey could never quite muster the same enthusiasm.

She jammed the key in the lock, twisting the doorknob open. A small white envelope sat wedged against the door frame. She pushed the inner door open, yet her feet remained glued in place, her eyes locked on the mysterious object. Her pulse kicked up a notch.

Maybe it was from someone else—someone other than whoever had left the copy last night. She squatted, reaching for the envelope. Heavier than last night's, it appeared to be similar, a plain number ten, this one unsealed.

Lindsey stood, easing the flap of the envelope open by the edge, doing her best not to leave her own prints. Gold glimmered inside the envelope. A ring, delicate and old, small gems set in the shape of a heart. She flashed on an image of a family picnic, sitting holding hands with her mother, lovingly touching the heirloom ruby ring.

This ring.

Lindsey's heart squeezed. *Someone knew.* Somewhere out there, someone knew exactly what had happened to her mother and was reaching out. Perhaps that same someone knew where her body had been dumped.

Matt Alessandro had been correct. Lindsey had spent her entire adult life wondering why her mother had been murdered. The trial had yielded nothing but professions of innocence from Matt's father, even though the jury had found him guilty.

Lindsey needed more. She yearned to find out exactly what had happened, and why. To do that, she had to find out who had left this ring and the photocopied license last night.

She stepped through the door, determined to find a suitable plastic bag to protect the ring and any prints. Focused on the envelope in her hand and the glimmer of gold inside, she thought her mind was playing tricks when a shadow fell across her own on the threshold.

A pair of hands shoved her forward before she could react, before the reality of what was happening could register. She toppled over, striking the side of her skull against the marble top of a table. Pain exploded as she fell to the cool floor. Everything faded—sound, light, thought.

Lindsey's world turned to black.

Chapter Two

Matt had always had a bit of a temper. He could admit it. Hell, he came by it honestly, yet not from his dad. From his mother. The woman was a hothead the likes of which South Philly would probably never see again.

Be that as it may, right now every deep breathing trick he knew did nothing to calm the frustration ignited by his visit to Lindsey Tarlington.

How could she stare at him like an ice princess and pretend she didn't care about the package she'd been left? She had to care. *Had* to.

How could she not?

By all accounts, Lindsey had dedicated her life to helping others solve mysteries. Her mother's disappearance had been one of the biggest mysteries to ever hit the region.

Of course, Lindsey believed his father had been the murderer. Matt believed anything but. Now, he had only to convince her to listen to him.

The light at the intersection ahead changed from

yellow to red. He slowed his SUV to a stop and glared at the notes tossed on the seat beside him.

He knew where the woman lived. That's probably where she'd gone. The little blond guard at the office hadn't offered any information when he'd called back other than that Lindsey had left shortly after their meeting.

He knew he'd gotten to her. The facts plain didn't add up. He was no detective, but he wasn't stupid. And, neither was Lindsey Tarlington.

He pulled a U-turn when the light turned green, headed back toward the other side of town.

Matt glanced down at the address scribbled on a scrap of paper. Fifty-two Elm. How very suburban.

His father's conviction had shattered his mother's dream of escaping the city to move across the river to New Jersey.

Bitter anger rekindled in Matt's gut, like a slow-burning ember he could never quite put out. He blinked, willing the heat to go away. It wasn't Lindsey Tarlington's fault he and his family had lost everything trying to defend his father. It was the system's fault. The system he now worked to keep fair.

Fifteen minutes later, he pulled to a stop in front of the house. A bright blue compact car sat in the drive.

He eased out of his truck, straightening to his full height. His father had not killed Camille Tarlington. The killer had gone free and, for some reason, had chosen to wait seventeen years to resurface. Matt intended to find out why—and who.

He climbed the center steps, rapping the brass knocker loudly against the weathered wooden door.

Something sounded inside, and he pressed his ear to the cool surface, trying to make out the noise.

Not a voice, but a moan. A whimper.

"Ms. Tarlington."

The noise sounded again, this time even more faint.

Matt tried the doorknob and it turned, unlocked. He pushed open the door, stepping inside as he did so.

Lindsey lay facedown, her black hair splayed across the marble foyer.

He dropped to his knees, sliding to a stop next to her motionless body. He checked for a pulse. Solid.

"Ms. Tarlington." He brushed several silken strands from her colorless face.

Matt's gut caught, twisting hard. Had the killer done this? He glanced around the foyer, from archway to archway, all leading to other areas of the large house where the attacker might still lurk.

He should search. He should get Lindsey out of the house. He should do more than just hold her, but at the moment, his instincts told him that's exactly what she needed. His instincts also told him whoever had done this was long gone.

Matt pulled his cell phone from his pocket, punching in 9-1-1 then quickly giving the address and details to the dispatcher. With his free hand, he reached for Lindsey's, intertwining her slender, soft fingers with his own.

Protectiveness hummed to life deep within him—a

determination to find whoever had done this and make sure he never had the chance again.

Lindsey's lush black lashes fluttered against her pale cheeks and she moaned, the sound nothing more than a soft cry. Matt pressed his lips close to her ear, inhaling her soft floral scent. "Stay still. Help's coming."

"Shoved me." The words slipped over her lips, like the murmurings of a sleepwalker.

"Don't try to talk." Matt squeezed her hand tighter, willing her to hang on.

Her eyes flashed open like huge saucers of sky, frightened, slowly focusing on his face.

"It's Matt Alessandro. You're safe now."

"You shoved me."

Lindsey's accusation slammed him like an oncoming freight train. "No." He shook his head as he uttered the one-word response, stunned she could think him capable.

A shadow of doubt glazed her stare, and reality settled in, chilling Matt to the core.

Lindsey Tarlington eyed him as if he were a killer's son, but then, why wouldn't she?

In her eyes, he was.

LINDSEY WOKE TO THE sensation of someone squeezing her hand. Rugged male features flashed through her mind. Hazel eyes. Sharp jaw. Piercing gaze.

Matt Alessandro.

Fear seized her, and she jerked her arm, trying to free herself from his grip.

"Hey, hey." A soothing male voice slipped into her

consciousness. Familiar. Gruff. "Who you fighting now, peanut?"

She forced open her eyes, relief coursing through her as she met the familiar, yet concerned, pale gray eyes. "Uncle Frank?"

He leaned to press a kiss to her temple.

"It must be bad if they dragged you away from city hall."

His warm laughter rumbled through the small room. "At least that wit of yours is still intact."

Pain pulsed through Lindsey's skull. She could remember the moment of impact but nothing after. She scanned the room, taking in the small, sterile details. Chrome, tile, plastic. The walls and floor a bland mixture of teal and cream. "Where am I?"

"Cooper Hospital." Her uncle's voice had gone uncharacteristically gentle. "Doctor says you'll be fine. They're going to keep you overnight, but there's nothing to worry about."

"What happened?"

Her uncle shook his head, his features falling slack. "Matt Alessandro found you, Lindsey. He took care of you until help got there. You really took a fall."

Alessandro? A fall? Lindsey's pulse quickened. "He shoved me from behind."

"Why on earth would you think that?"

"I felt him."

"Did you see him?"

Lindsey rankled at the disbelief palpable in her uncle's voice. "I saw a shadow."

"You were unconscious when Alessandro found you. Maybe you simply blacked out. Only thought you saw a shadow."

Incredulity flooded through her. "You can't believe that."

He nodded, his pale gaze narrowing in an obvious attempt at sympathy.

"What about the ring?"

Her uncle frowned, tiny creases framing his surprised stare. "Ring?"

"Mommy's ring? I found it right before I was attacked."

The lines of his face deepened. "There was no ring. No evidence that anyone had been in your house. We had our best team out there just to be sure. You fell, peanut."

She shook her head, wincing as a fresh band of pain wrapped its fingers around the side of her skull. "You missed it then. Her ring was there in an envelope."

"No." His tone dropped to the low, all-business timbre she'd dreaded ever since he'd married into the family. "No ring, honey."

Lindsey swallowed, unable to believe her uncle would doubt her word. "Then someone took it." She struggled to sit up, but had to settle for merely shifting against the pillows, too sore to do anything more. "Whoever shoved me took it."

Anger flashed across his now stern features. "Tony Alessandro took your mother's ring seventeen years ago." He squeezed her hand. "I'd like to find the monster who left you that copy last night. It's brought back your old nightmares."

Frustration mixed with the fear churning in Lindsey's stomach. The nightmares had started the night her mother disappeared. The blackouts had begun a few weeks later. What had happened today had been neither. "This wasn't a nightmare."

Her uncle's forced smile crinkled the lines framing his eyes. "I'll go get Aunt Pris. She's been waiting outside."

He stood to leave, but Lindsey tightened her fingers around his, determination filling her with strength. "I saw Mommy's ring."

Her uncle extracted his hand then pushed away from the hospital bed. "You've had a shock. You only thought you saw it."

Lindsey stared at his back in disbelief. She had no doubt about what had happened. She'd been attacked. The only question was by whom? And what had happened to her mother's ring?

If Uncle Frank wasn't going to help her find the answers, she'd find them on her own.

MATT SHIFTED AGAINST THE stiff back of the waiting room chair, doing his best to ignore the nonstop glare Lindsey Tarlington's aunt, Priscilla Bell, had been channeling in his direction.

The mayor's wife had always kept a low profile, but she hadn't been seen in public in months. Based on her appearance, the rumors about her health might be true.

She looked like hell. Thin, frail, sickly. Perhaps being married to the mighty Frank Bell had taken a toll.

When Mayor Bell emerged from Lindsey's room and huddled with his wife, Matt discreetly stared at the floor. He did his best to pick up scraps of their conversation, but they kept their voices too low for him to make out their words.

Frank Bell. Matt fought the urge to snarl at the man.

Bell had been a hotshot in the district attorney's office at the time Lindsey's mother, the D.A.'s younger daughter, had disappeared. Convicting Matt's father had catapulted Bell's career onto the fast track. Of course, the fact he'd been married to the D.A.'s older daughter, Priscilla, hadn't hurt, either. And now political rumblings had Bell setting his sights on a quick trip from mayor of Haddontowne to governor of New Jersey.

As a public defender, Matt had butted heads with the man on more than one occasion. One thing was for certain—Frank Bell had the tenacity of a pit bull terrier. If he wanted the governor's mansion, he'd let nothing get in his way—including any doubts about the conviction that had made his career.

"Thought you would have left by now." Bell's voice carried across the small waiting room from where he stood next to the chair his wife had vacated.

Matt stood, fully aware he'd adopted an antagonistic stance. He'd learned a long time ago that head-on was the smartest way to address the mighty Mayor Bell. "Wanted to make sure your niece was all right."

"She'll be a lot better off if she doesn't see you here." Bell turned away, but barked out over his shoulder. "Maybe you should be paying attention to your clients and leaving my niece alone."

"She deserves to know her mother's killer got away scot-free."

Bell pivoted, unchecked hatred seething from his battleship-gray glare. Bitterness swirled in Matt's gut. No wonder his father's defense had never had a chance. If Frank Bell had managed half of the fury he was projecting now, the jury would have been terrified to do anything but return a guilty verdict.

"My niece sleeps just fine at night knowing the man who killed her mother met his just end in jail."

"But you never found the body. How can you be so sure?"

"Evidence doesn't lie."

"No, but it can be conveniently interpreted for a quick conviction." Matt fought to hold his anger in check. "You and I both know this topic isn't closed, Mayor. Whoever sent that copy and attacked your niece is determined to reopen old wounds."

He turned sharply on one heel, stepping toward the elevator, determined to have the last word. For once.

"My niece fell, Mr. Alessandro." Bell's words stopped Matt cold. "The shock of seeing her mother's ID was too much for her. If I find out you're behind any of this, you'll pay."

"How can you—" Matt spun to argue, but Bell had disappeared back into the treatment room.

Fell. Could the man honestly believe that? Lindsey Tarlington had been certain she'd been shoved when Matt found her, and he saw no reason to doubt her story.

So why did Frank Bell? Maybe believing his niece complicated Bell's plans for the governor's mansion.

Matt punched the elevator button, hot emotion rolling through his veins. He believed Lindsey's story, and he planned to tell her so—in person.

Her attack might present just the opportunity he needed to begin earning the woman's trust.

THE NEXT AFTERNOON, LINDSEY stood in the middle of the attic studio, deserted since the night her mother had vanished. She closed her eyes, trying to sense her mother's presence, wishing fervently for a sign or a clue as to what had happened all those years ago.

Lindsey had been discharged from the hospital just a few hours earlier, sent on her way with a mild concussion, nothing more. The doctor had agreed with the police that her pounding head was consistent with an accidental fall.

A disbelieving laugh burst from her lips. Fall, her foot. There was no way she'd confuse being shoved with falling.

Even more discouraging had been Uncle Frank's phone call. The photocopy of her mother's license had been made on paper found in any office supply store. There had been nothing distinguishing to provide a clue. Nothing. Not a single fingerprint or fiber.

The house below her creaked, and she flinched, even though she'd checked and double-checked every door and window before she'd pulled down the old attic steps and made the climb up to what had been her mother's sanctuary.

Lindsey hadn't been up here in recent years. Any time the urge had sneaked into her mind, she'd ignored it, choosing instead to pretend the space didn't exist. Sometimes avoidance was easier to face than the truth.

She opened her eyes to take in the sight. The attic remained as it had always been, a small art studio, lovingly filled with her mother's work and favorite things.

Lindsey stepped gingerly toward the easel that stood off to one corner. She fingered the wooden shape, draped in an old sheet, then stood back, watching dust particles dance in the beam of sunlight forcing its way through the streaked attic window.

One thing had never made sense to her, even as a child. If, as the prosecution had claimed, her mother had been in love with Tony Alessandro and her murder the result of a lover's quarrel gone horribly wrong, wouldn't there have been some trace of the affair here in her mother's retreat? Wouldn't there have been a letter? A photo? Something. Anything.

Lindsey sank to the plank wood flooring. She'd searched this space relentlessly as a teen, until her father had begged her to stop. The pain of her mother's death and supposed infidelity had been more than the once-vibrant man could endure.

He'd never been the same after that stormy night.

When he died four years later in a one-car crash, during a late spring thunderstorm, the residents of Haddontowne had murmured suicide.

Emotional pain engulfed her, threatening to squeeze the air from her lungs. How could her father have made that choice? How could he have left her alone?

The doorbell rang, and Lindsey swore softly under her breath. She stood quickly and her vision swam, an unwanted reminder of the blow she'd taken to her head. She glared at the attic steps.

Climbing up the unsteady staircase had been a challenge. Climbing down in time to catch the door would probably be the death of her. A chill tap-danced up her spine, and she shuddered.

She had to stop expecting the worst.

Carefully, she set one foot and then the other on the ancient rungs, the springs and hinges squeaking and groaning as she descended. When she hit the hallway floor, she hurried toward the downstairs, ignoring the pounding in her skull and leaving the attic stairs down behind her.

It would be easier to leave them unfolded than to wrestle them up and down each time she went searching. And she had every intention of searching her mother's studio again.

Just as it had when she'd been younger, her gut told her something lay hidden in that space—something that would unlock the mystery of exactly how her mother had died.

"Who is it?" she called out as she hit the foyer.

"Matt Alessandro."

Lindsey's breath caught. She stopped in her tracks, unsure whether or not to open the door and unable to coax additional words from her mouth.

"I came to see how you were." Matt's deep voice rumbled through the heavy old wood. "I was worried about you."

Disbelief fired in her belly as she reached for the knob. "You were worried about—" The sight of him froze her last word on her lips.

Genuine concern painted his features. His gaze bore through her, kicking an unwanted curiosity to life. Soft creases lined his forehead as he raked one strong hand through his too-long hair. He straightened from where he'd been leaning against the doorjamb.

"Took you a while to answer. You okay?"

The soft timbre of his question reached inside her, testing emotional walls that hadn't been breached in years. The man seemed sincere. Was it possible?

"You could have called." Lindsey stood in the doorway, unable to will her feet to step aside to let him in. Perhaps it was best to keep him outside on the step, where a stranger belonged.

"How's your head?" He stepped toward her, and Lindsey instinctively backed up.

"They think I fell."

His eyes narrowed, now appearing more brown than green. "I think you believe that as much as I do."

Lindsey swallowed, forcing her focus away from

the expression that made him appear human rather than a monster's son.

"May I come in?" His tone dropped low, sending a ripple of trepidation across her shoulders.

She hesitated, zeroing in on the folder he hugged between his elbow and side. "What's that?"

"Something you need to see."

"Listen, if you still want to hire me—"

Alessandro shook his head. "I want to help you."

Confusion swirled in the pit of Lindsey's stomach. She raised her gaze to his, only to find herself pinned by the intensity of his stare. "Can I trust you, Mr. Alessandro?"

"Yes." He answered without hesitation.

The protective lock deep inside her eased ever so slightly. She took a step backward, pulling the door wide and tipping her head toward the foyer. Alessandro followed the nonverbal invitation, stepping over the threshold.

"Thanks for your help yesterday." The hesitant tone of Lindsey's voice surprised her.

Yet, it wasn't intimidation Matt's presence had sparked to life, but rather alertness. The sounds and scents surrounding Lindsey had become more vibrant, more vital. Perhaps the sensation could be attributed to her defense mechanisms kicking into high gear. Surely that explained the way his nearness made her feel.

Matt held out the folder, the flap secured by a worn rubber band. "I'm just glad you're all right." He studied her then, as if memorizing each detail of her face. He lifted his hand toward the bruise that marred the side of her face. "You were lucky."

Heat flushed Lindsey's neck, and she pointed to the folder to deflect his focus. "What's this?"

"Case file." He dropped his hand. "Buddy of mine made copies for me a while back. Not exactly on the up-and-up, so I'd appreciate it if you didn't say anything to your uncle."

Excitement swelled in her core. "My mother's case file?"

Matt nodded, pressing the folder into her hands.

She let it sit on top of her palms momentarily, before curling her fingers around the edges. "I've asked for this, but my uncle told me it had disappeared."

Matt's tone softened. "He probably wanted to spare you, but I thought you deserved to see it."

She lifted her focus to his, again jolted by the intensity of his scrutiny. "Why?"

"Because the clue to whatever really happened to your mother is somewhere in here. I've been over this too many times to count, but you..." He looked down at the folder then retrained his stare on Lindsey.

Her stomach somersaulted, dread and anticipation tangling. The documentation represented the thing she wanted—yet feared—the most. The full story behind that awful night.

"You may be able to spot something here that no one else has. And someone's waited until now to pull you in." Matt shrugged again. "Maybe together we can make some sense of this."

Lindsey swallowed, battling her desire to trust him and the reality of his identity. She had no doubt Matt's father had killed her mother, but she'd never understood why. She'd never believed her mother had been involved with Tony Alessandro as anything other than a coworker.

"A jury convicted your father, Mr. Alessandro. I can understand your interest in trying to find a way to prove him innocent, but I harbor no doubts. I know my mother's killer went to prison and died there."

Pain flashed across Matt's features as he patted the folder. "Evaluate this. Then make your decision. That's all I ask." He turned toward the door, hesitating before he headed outside. "My family was destroyed unjustly, Ms. Tarlington. Someone out there knows something. You know it, and I know it. I intend to find out what that something is."

Lindsey fought down the anguish clawing its way out from the recesses of her mind. "Your father murdered my mother." She spoke the words softly, flatly, as if the slightest exertion might cause more pain than she could handle. She straightened, the strength of her certainty flooding through her. "I don't lie awake at night worrying about how that might have affected your family."

Matt pressed his lips tightly together before speaking. "I don't expect you to believe me now, but I know your reputation. You like the whole story. You evaluate each of your cases from every possible angle. Am I right?"

Lindsey nodded, her pulse pounding in her ears.

Matt pointed toward the folder. "Your mother deserves that same attention. Her real killer's still out there."

Lindsey said nothing as he stepped from the brick steps to the center walk. His suit jacket fit trim across his broad shoulders, narrowing down to his slender hips. Confidence emanated from each solid footstep he took, shoulders squared, head held high. He looked nothing like she imagined the son of a murderer would.

She tightened her grip on the folder. Did she want to know what lay inside? A calm resignation whispered through her. She did, and Matt Alesssandro knew it.

She felt compelled to believe him when she wanted to do anything but. The reality was that his doubts and questions tapped into her own need to know the truth.

"Did you see the ring?" she called out suddenly, her voice contrasting sharply against the quiet of the neighborhood.

Matt stopped partway down the walk, turning to face her. The play of the late-day sun against the angles of his face momentarily stole her breath. His chestnut hair fluttered in the breeze. "What ring?"

"I found it before I was hit." Hope coursed through her. "It was in a plain, white envelope. My mother's ring."

He narrowed his stare, frowning. "The only thing I found was you. No envelope." He shook his head. "No ring. I'm sorry." He nodded toward the folder in her arms. "Was it the ring she was wearing that night?"

Lindsey nodded. "She never took it off."

"All the more reason for you to review that. I'll stop by your office tomorrow. We'll go forward from there."

As she watched his SUV ease away from the curb, anxiety and doubt coiled deep inside her.

We'll go forward from there.

No matter what her instincts told her, Matt Alessandro was the son of the monster who had murdered her mother.

She must be insane.

Chapter Three

Matt pulled his SUV into the parking lot outside the Polaris Group office and gripped the steering wheel, shooting up one last prayer Lindsey Tarlington would see things his way.

She had to.

He scrubbed a hand across his face, sighing at the feel of wiry stubble beneath his fingers. Damn, he'd forgotten to shave. Again.

He'd been up all night laying the groundwork for a case pending against a local gang member. The kid might not be an honor roll candidate, but Matt had no doubt he'd been set up to take the rap in a burglary charge. He had no intention of letting his obsession with clearing his father's name affect the representation of his clients.

After he'd finished the necessary paperwork, he'd spent the early morning hours poring over the extra copy he'd made of Camille Tarlington's file. Everything seemed in order—had always seemed in order—except he knew his father was no killer. More so, his father had never been unfaithful to his mother. The prosecution had used the alleged love affair between Camille and Tony Alessandro to provide motive and intent. The theory wasn't possible.

Matt shook his head. Tony had been a gentle man who had turned his love of the outdoors into a thriving floral business with shops in Philadelphia and New Jersey. Matt struggled to remember a single night his father had come home without a bouquet of handpicked flowers for his mother. He couldn't think of one.

Yet Tony Alessandro had been convicted of a violent murder. A murder in which the body had never been found. His conviction had been based on blood spatter found in Camille's station wagon and on the murder weapon found inside the shop. That, combined with testimony about the alleged affair, had been enough to send Matt's father away, where a fellow inmate had fatally stabbed him six months later.

Matt's chest ached. It seemed like yesterday, and yet it seemed a lifetime ago.

He pushed open the driver's door and unfurled himself from his vehicle, heading straight for Lindsey Tarlington's office. Common courtesy dictated Matt should have phoned before dropping by, but he'd never been one to worry much about common courtesy.

Look how far it had gotten his dad.

No. Matt had been well served by the element of surprise during his time in the public defender's office. He could see no reason to treat Lindsey Tarlington any differently than he treated any other client or source.

Her pale gaze flashed through his mind's eye, and his gut tightened. He shoved down the unwanted protective urge.

Whoever had left Camille Tarlington's photocopied driver's license was obviously privy to her personal effects, and perhaps much, much more. The possibility of clearing his father's name loomed more closely on the horizon than it ever had. Matt wasn't about to go soft just because of Lindsey's vulnerable expression.

If she'd reviewed the contents of the file he'd given her, Lindsey would have to agree something seemed off, because while the case against his father appeared to be neat and tidy, it reeked of convenience. There was no way Matt would sacrifice his father's memory and good name for someone else's benefit.

LINDSEY SWALLOWED DOWN another mouthful of burnt coffee then rolled her shoulders. She'd been up all night staring at the horrific words and images captured in her mother's case file.

It would be a miracle if she ever slept again. If the cold, hard facts didn't bring back her nightmares, nothing would.

She looked across at her partners, Tally Cooke and Regina Payne, who sat, along with their office manager, Patty Jones, intently staring at the notes, reports and photos spread across the office's conference table.

Each had a full plate right now, clients who needed help with cold cases or ongoing investigations, but

Lindsey knew her partners' input would be invaluable in talking out her mother's case.

Tally was a whiz at logic—possessing an uncanny ability to analyze a puzzle or series of clues. Regina had a nose for the law and saw the world in black and white. Lindsey had always been the taskmaster, keeping the group on schedule and on track. How ironic that she now pulled their focus from their paying case work to her personal crusade.

"I never believed she was having an affair." Lindsey shrugged. "I can't accept that."

"Why not?" Tally's sharp tone jolted Lindsey from her fog of exhaustion.

Lindsey shrugged. "She loved my father." Her chest tightened. "She wasn't the type to cheat."

Tally raised an auburn brow. "You were twelve years old. You'd have no idea if your mother was cheating."

"She loved us." Hadn't she?

Doubt pooled in Lindsey's stomach. She'd searched her mother's art studio again in the early morning hours, after reading testimony detailing her mother's adulterous liaison with Tony Alessandro. Her intuition screamed her mother hadn't cheated on her father. She just wasn't sure if that intuition came from Lindsey the daughter, the woman or the truth-seeker. She only knew it came—hard and sure.

Her voice grew more determined. "She never cheated on my father." And if she hadn't been involved with Tony Alessandro, why had he killed her? If he had killed her.

Lindsey shoved down the doubt. She wasn't ready to follow that train of thought—to imagine her mother's killer had gone free.

Silence beat for several seconds among the four women.

"Did your parents ever argue?" Regina's gaze had narrowed, now matching the disbelieving expression Tally wore.

Lindsey shook her head. "Never." She caught herself. "I mean, no more than any other married couple."

While she hated the sympathy painted across her friends' faces, she'd learned to ignore the pity a long time ago. She flashed on the memory of her father, taking her back to church for the first time after her mother had disappeared. "Keep your chin up, Lindsey. Don't ever let them think you're weak."

She hoisted her chin now. "They had regrets, but doesn't every couple? You have to believe me on this. She wouldn't have cheated on my father. She loved him."

"Why did the investigation focus on that?" Tally's tone had gone all business, her specialty.

Lindsey ran her hand across the copies, wishing they'd yielded more than they had. "One of my mother's coworkers claimed it was true." She moved her hand from the papers to her face. She blinked back the fatigue that had seeped into her every bone many hours ago. "Her name was Lorraine Mickle. She came forward voluntarily, and the prosecution latched on to a crime of passion theory as the basis for their case."

Tally's eyes had narrowed, as had Regina's. "There's no proof other than her word?"

Lindsey blew out a frustrated breath. "No proof of their affair. No letters. No phone messages. No gifts. I've never found anything in her studio, either." She frowned. "It's like my uncle's office built the case on the strength of one witness plus the circumstantial evidence and ran it in for a touchdown." The touchdown that had shot Frank Bell's political star into the stratosphere and sent Tony Alessandro to his death. Again, Lindsey swallowed down the doubt that nagged at her.

"Sometimes that's all it takes." Regina shrugged.

"What's the hard evidence?" Tally gestured toward the folder.

Lindsey flipped through the papers until she found the crime scene report. "Large quantity of blood in the car, blood spatter consistent with that from a major artery, matching blood type found on a pair of floral shears in the shop with Alessandro's fingerprints on it."

"The shears could have been planted." Patty's serious gaze widened.

"You've been watching too much television," Tally mumbled.

"Maybe you shouldn't be questioning this at all," Regina offered. "You have to admit the physical evidence is compelling. Don't let the son convince you to stir this up if you don't want to."

Lindsey sighed. Seventy-two hours earlier her mother's death had been nothing more than a horrible part of her past. Now it had pushed front and center in her every waking thought. Much of that had to do with Matt Alessandro, the case file he'd given her and his un-flinching determination. Her stomach flip-flopped at the remembered intensity of his gaze.

Yet, truth was, the horror of her mother's death had come back to life because of the photocopied license someone had left in her door. And the ring. The ring that had disappeared during a broad daylight attack every-one seemed to doubt.

Everyone except Matt Alessandro.

"What about the driver's license?" She lifted her focus to her partners' faces, deciding to leave the ring out of the discussion for now. Tally and Regina both blew out sighs and sat back against their chairs.

"Damn," Tally muttered.

"Someone's got information that's not in these files." Lindsey squeezed her eyes shut then snapped them open, straightening in her seat. "I need to find out what that is, even if the conclusion remains the same."

"It does all seem fairly circumstantial." Regina's features had tightened and she nodded, meeting Lind-sey's stare head on.

"Okay." Tally jumped to her feet, pacing a tight pattern behind Regina's chair. "So where do we start?" She gestured into the empty air above her head. "Let's try to forget this is your mother we're talking about. What would we do first? What puzzle piece would we go after?"

"We'd question how thorough the searches were. If Alessandro was guilty, why was nothing found at his house? What other explanations could be given for the evidence found at the store?" Lindsey straightened. "And why give so much weight to the testimony of Lorraine Mickle?"

Regina leaned forward across the table. Tally had stopped pacing. Both stared intently at Lindsey.

"So?" Regina prodded.

"First, I'll find Mickle and talk to her." Lindsey sucked in a deep breath, determination edging out the doubt that had filled her moments earlier. "Then, I'll question my uncle about how they conducted this investigation." She looked from Tally, to Regina, to Patty, who had dropped into Tally's vacant chair. "I'm going to find out exactly what happened to my mother."

"I never doubted you would."

The rich, male rumble sent the hairs at the nape of Lindsey's neck tingling to attention. She knew the source before she turned. Sheer, unmasked appreciation glimmered in her friends' eyes.

Matt Alessandro stood just inside the door. They'd been so engrossed in their conversation that not one of them had heard him enter. Lindsey held her breath, amazed by the impact the man had on her senses. The now familiar and unwanted edginess slid through her system at the mere sight of him.

He crossed the room, snagging a spare chair from Tally's cubicle and positioning it between Regina and Lindsey at the small table. His gaze never left Lindsey's. Not for a moment.

"So." One dark brow arched. "When do we start?"

"I'M RELIEVED TO HEAR you agree with me."

Matt stole a glance at Lindsey Tarlington's profile and body language as she perched on the passenger seat of his SUV. She'd been as anxious to speak with Lorraine Mickle as he had been, and now she sat next to him as he drove toward Mickle's home.

If he didn't know better, he'd think the leather seat had given her a shock. The woman was obviously ill at ease as his passenger.

"I never said I agreed with you, Mr. Alessandro."

"Matt." He turned to face her.

She returned his look, her dark brows lifting, as if he'd surprised her. "Matt," she repeated softly.

The sound of his name on her lips sent a spiral of appreciation coiling tight inside his gut. Not good. He had no time to become interested in anything about Lindsey Tarlington other than her investigative brain. From what he'd heard over the years, her intellect was her best feature.

He bit back a grin as she tugged the hem of her skirt over her shapely knees. Whoever had made the intellect observation obviously hadn't been a red-blooded male.

Matt retrained his attention on the road, focusing on what she'd just said. "I heard you say you don't believe the file contents are conclusive."

"No." She tapped a hand along the passenger door. "You heard me say I wanted to investigate further. I still believe your father killed my mother."

He drew in a steady breath, doing his best to avoid losing his temper. "That's insane."

"Really?"

Out of the corner of his eye he could see her watching him, scrutinizing his reaction.

"The physical evidence points to your father. The jury obviously agreed. The thing I can't accept is the affair between your father and my mother." She made a snapping noise with her tongue. "No way."

He narrowed his gaze, hoping he hadn't been wrong about Lindsey's nose for the truth. "At least we agree on one thing. That's a start."

"So you don't believe they were involved?"

Her voice had suddenly lost its edge, and Matt felt himself softening. "I never did."

They drove the next few moments in uncomfortable silence. He broke the void first. "We need to have a goal for this visit. I'm a big believer in all parties being on the same page."

"And what page are you on, Mr. Aless—Matt?"

"I'm on the page that thinks Mickle was a convenient witness—a convenient witness with a tidy little story your uncle never questioned." He shot her a glance. Color fired in her cheeks. So, he'd hit a nerve. "What page are you on, Ms. Tarlington?"

The light ahead turned yellow and he slowed the truck to a stop, turning to focus fully on the woman beside him.

"Call me Lindsey."

He nodded.

She frowned then spoke. "I'm on the page that agrees Mickle's testimony seemed a bit convenient, and had no evidentiary proof of any kind."

Matt widened his gaze and nodded. "Very good." The light shifted to green, and he pressed the truck forward. "Maybe we're not so far apart in our thinking after all."

"What's *your* goal for our visit?"

"My goal..." He mulled the question, taking his time before he answered. His goal was to have Lindsey realize reasonable doubt existed about his father's guilt, but as far as she needed to know...? "My goal is to find the crack in Mickle's story. Fair enough?"

Lindsey nodded. "Fair enough."

NERVOUS ANTICIPATION FLUTTERED to life in Lindsey's chest as Matt pulled the SUV to a stop at the entrance to a gated neighborhood. An elderly guard leaned forward through the casement window of the small guardhouse. "Name?"

"Matt Alessandro."

"Here to see?"

"Lorraine Mickle. Forty-two Hemingway."

"She expecting you?"

"Yes."

Lindsey held her tongue as the gate lifted.

The guard tipped his cap. "Have a good visit."

"Thank you." Smile lines creased Matt's cheeks as he grinned. "We plan to."

"Very smooth," Lindsey said softly as the SUV cleared the gate.

"Please." Matt's grin deepened. "I'm quite certain you didn't earn your reputation without bending the rules a time or two."

"Reputation?" Lindsey smiled, unable to resist the teasing tone of Matt's voice.

"It never ceases to amaze me how people will welcome you simply because you act like you know what you're doing." Matt cast a quick glance in her direction and her stomach caught.

She nodded in agreement, saying nothing, not trusting her voice to be steady at that moment. After all, hadn't she done that very thing when she'd opened her front door to this man just yesterday? She'd welcomed him into her home because he'd been so self-assured.

"Amazing," Matt repeated, holding her gaze for another second before refocusing on the road.

Lindsey turned her own attention to Hemingway Lane as he eased the truck into the turn. Lorraine Mickle. The woman on whom the motive portion of the case against Matt's father had hinged. The woman who had seen Tony Alessandro and Camille Tarlington in a lover's argument.

Allegedly.

Matt pulled the truck into a driveway, and Lindsey fought the shiver that slithered its way up her spine. Her gaze landed on a gaudy mailbox painted to resemble a pink flamingo. Number forty-two.

"Ready?"

His voice broke her trance.

"Ready." She gripped her briefcase and climbed

from the truck, headed toward what she hoped would be answers to the questions that had come back to life after seventeen years of silence.

Composed was the only word Lindsey could think of to describe the look painted on Lorraine Mickle's face as she opened the door. If she didn't know better, Lindsey would swear Mickle had been expecting them. The woman showed not an ounce of surprise as they introduced themselves.

Mickle's blond hair had been twisted artfully into a bun at the nape of her neck. Her ivory skin showed subtle lines of age, but she was a lovely woman. Lindsey's best guess would put Mickle's age somewhere around forty. A smattering of fine lines framed her pale green eyes, but her features remained sharp, her jaw and neck flawless, like those of a much younger woman.

"I've just put on a pot of coffee, can I get you both a cup?"

Matt and Lindsey exchanged a quick glance. "Thank you," Lindsey answered. Matt nodded his agreement.

The small ranch, though cozy, could only be described as immaculate. Lindsey had the sense she'd stepped into a decorating magazine photo spread, surrounded by carefully selected furnishings and decorations.

Mickle disappeared through a doorway into the kitchen and returned a few moments later, a coffee cup in each hand. "I apologize for my appearance." She nodded to the emerald-green velour robe she wore. "You caught me getting ready to take a shower."

"We apologize for not calling first," Matt said.

Lindsey couldn't help but be impressed by the sincere expression he wore.

"No problem. I'm always happy to have company." Mickle's expression remained welcoming. "Would you like to take a seat?"

Matt shook his head. Lindsey mirrored the move. Both remained where they stood, each now holding a steaming cup. "We don't plan to stay long, Ms. Mickle," Matt said. "We appreciate you seeing us."

"No problem." The woman's face broke into a gracious smile. "What can I do for you?"

"I wonder if I could ask you a few questions about the night Camille Tarlington disappeared? We understand you and she worked together at my father's floral shop."

Lorraine's smile tightened as she nodded. "Yes. We did. Horrible tragedy."

"Why were you so quick to suggest my father and Mrs. Tarlington's alleged affair?"

The suddenness of Matt's question shocked Lindsey. She could only imagine how Lorraine Mickle must feel.

Yet the woman didn't bat an eye. "There was nothing alleged about it. Anyone who knew them knew they shared something intimate. When the police questioned me about anyone Camille had argued with, Tony…your father…immediately came to mind."

Lindsey's pulse quickened. According to the notes she'd read, Mickle had come forward. She hadn't been asked about a possible motive because she'd offered the information first.

Matt closed the gap between him and Mickle. His features tensed. "I'm confused. You were questioned regarding the argument?"

Mickle frowned but stood her ground. "I thought you asked me about what I told them."

"I did." Matt nodded. He said nothing additional. Lindsey realized he was giving the woman just enough rope to hang herself.

Mickle glanced from Matt to Lindsey. Lindsey sipped her coffee and smiled, waiting patiently for the answer.

"I misspoke." Mickle's confident smile returned and she chuckled softly. "It's been a long time, you need to remember I'm not as young as I used to be." She nodded as if the memory had suddenly come into focus. "I did tell the police about the argument. I thought the information might help."

She focused her attention on Matt. "Your father had a quick temper. I heard him arguing in the back room with Camille. He left the shop shortly after she went out on a late delivery." She shook her head. "Camille never returned, and the police came to see me the next day after your father," she said, nodding in Lindsey's direction, "reported she'd never come home."

The acid taste of coffee burned Lindsey's throat. She'd never forget that night, or the way her father had paced from room to room, from window to window, after he'd returned from his weekly bowling league and found Camille not at home.

"So you offered the information about the argument, correct?" Matt asked, his tone intent and stern.

Mickle nodded. "Just as I said."

Matt narrowed his eyes. "You may have heard some new evidence has come forward. Ms. Tarlington and I had questions and thought it best to seek you out. We apologize for any inconvenience."

He shot a glance at Lindsey, his expression softening as their gazes met. She nodded then smiled at Mickle.

"I just can't imagine why you'd want to dredge up the past." Mickle clucked her tongue. "It was a horrible time for both of your families."

"Yes, but I've always wondered what they argued about." Matt's features had grown serious.

Mickle glanced at the front door, probably wondering why she'd opened her home to them in the first place. "I remember exactly. Your father wanted to go public with the affair and Camille refused."

Lindsey had enough experience with lying spouses, parents and children to read the nonverbal cues, yet Mickle's cues were yielding nothing. The woman seemed to be unreadable. Was it because Lindsey was too close to the case? Or was Mickle actually telling the truth? Had her mother been involved with Alessandro?

"You had no doubt they were lovers?" Matt stepped closer to where Lorraine stood. The woman shook her head, backed up one step, then held her place.

Apparently Matt's thoughts had followed the same progression as Lindsey's.

"More coffee?" Mickle's voice climbed perceptibly.

"No, thank you." Matt smiled. He nodded in Lindsey's direction. "Ms. Tarlington? More coffee?"

Lindsey shook her head. "None for me thanks." She glanced down into her half-full cup. "Matter of fact, I'll put these in the sink." She held out a hand for Matt's cup, wrapping her fingers tightly around the porcelain as he handed it to her. "We should probably get going."

Matt nodded, holding out a hand toward Mickle. "Right. We should let you get back to what you were doing. You've been most helpful."

As the woman shook hands with Matt, Lindsey stepped into the kitchen, but froze at the sight of an ornament hanging in the window over the sink. An angel. Handmade.

Her heart stuttered to a momentary stop before it began to race.

The last time she'd seen the angel it had been hanging from the rearview mirror of her mother's station wagon.

An icy chill built inside Lindsey, spreading to her arms and hands. Mickle appeared at her side, reaching for the cups, her expression full of concern. "Let me get those for you."

"You okay?" Lindsey sensed Matt's nearness behind her. His hand brushed against her shoulder, the sudden warmth a steadying force in the small, spinning room.

She handed the cups to Lorraine without taking her eyes from the ornament. "That was my mother's."

Mickle pivoted, following the direction of Lindsey's

gaze. "I'm sure there must be a million like it. You must be mistaken."

Lindsey crossed to the sink, stepping free of Matt's touch. She fingered the object, the sequins faded after all these years. She could still remember meticulously applying every single one—for her mother.

"I made it." The words escaped her in barely more than a whisper.

She lifted her focus to Mickle, who now stood next to her at the sink. The woman bobbled one coffee cup as she set it in the sink, the loud clatter filling the otherwise silent space. She nodded suddenly then tapped one finger to her chin. "You know that's right. I remember now. She gave it to me one day at work." Mickle shook her head, a sympathetic expression plastered across her face. "You take it, honey. She'd want you to have it."

Lindsey didn't hesitate. She plucked the ornament from its hanger, nodding her thanks to Mickle as she beelined for the front door.

"Thanks again for your time." Matt's words cut through the frenzied thoughts crowding Lindsey's mind. He cupped her elbow as they hurried toward his truck, steering her as if she were a lost child.

"My mother loved this. She would have never given it away." Her voice was unrecognizable with pent-up anger and frustration. "What's going on?"

"I'm not sure." Matt whirled Lindsey to face him, confidence flashing in his eyes. "But, we're going to find out."

"Her story was almost too smooth."

"Practiced." Matt nodded.

Or was it? Part of Lindsey believed Matt was right. If Mickle had been coached, there was a chance Tony Alessandro had been falsely accused. She'd clung to his guilt as gospel for the past seventeen years. Was she ready to consider another possibility?

The nagging questions at the base of her brain hammered relentlessly. Was Mickle lying? Or was she merely reciting the truth as she'd seen it seventeen years earlier? And who had left the photocopy—and the ring? And why?

Lindsey looked at Matt as his dark gaze bore into hers. Was his the determination of a killer's son, intent on clearing the family name no matter what the evidence showed? Or was his the face of a good man, secure in the knowledge of his father's innocence?

She swallowed down her growing turmoil. Only time would tell.

Chapter Four

Matt sat in front of what had once been his family's floral shop and sipped on a cup of stale coffee. He'd dropped Lindsey back at her office, having agreed to meet her later that evening to pore through the case file together.

While he'd wanted some time to analyze their conversation with Lorraine Mickle, he'd also wanted some time apart from Lindsey. When she'd first spotted her mother's ornament hanging from the kitchen window, his instinct had been to offer comfort. He'd had to hold himself back from pulling the woman into his arms—as if she'd let him.

Hell, the woman had spent the majority of her life certain his father had murdered her mother. Of all the women to inspire a sense of protectiveness, why her? Why now?

He didn't need a distraction, and he certainly didn't need one as lovely as Lindsey Tarlington. Maybe he should go forward alone, working through each piece of the puzzle, from Mickle's words to the old evidence. Checking and rechecking.

Certainty eased through him. A certainty that he needed Lindsey's help. He couldn't put his finger on it, but he knew she was the key to unlocking the truth about what had happened that night. Whoever had reached out to her with the photocopy of her mother's license had done so for a reason. Someone wanted the truth known, and had chosen Lindsey as the starting point.

Perhaps whoever had left the clue was someone with a bone to pick with Frank Bell.

Matt laughed, unable to hold in his sudden burst of breath. Who didn't have a bone to pick with Frank Bell? The man hadn't made many friends on his way from the D.A.'s office to the mayor's office. He'd never hesitated to step over or on top of anyone who got in his way.

Bell also seemed to be the master of putting people in the position of owing him a favor, and he never hesitated to call in those favors when he needed something done.

Matt gave a quick shake of his head then took another sip of coffee.

He needed to soften his obsession with Bell, no matter what his gut told him. If he'd learned nothing else during his time at the public defender's office, he'd learned to approach each case with an open mind and clean slate. Preconceived notions achieved nothing more than muddying the waters.

All he needed to do now was step back and look at Camille Tarlington's murder with a fresh perspective. He needed to start over.

From scratch.

With Lindsey's help.

Even though he'd been certain for seventeen years that Bell had played the leading role in railroading his father, he'd be wise to open his mind to the possibility of a different scenario. As long as he cleared his father's name, he didn't care who took the blame.

Matt drained the last of his coffee and peered again at the building that had once housed his father's pride and joy. His father's beautiful shop had become a pizza parlor, as if there wasn't already a pizza shop on every corner in this neck of South Jersey.

He checked the side mirror then eased his SUV away from the curb. He couldn't remember the last time he'd eaten, but suddenly he'd lost his appetite.

LINDSEY WATCHED FOR MATT to pull out of the lot before she turned away from her office door and climbed into her car. She had no plan to wait until she and Matt reviewed the evidence together. She needed a face-to-face with her uncle now.

Mickle's story had unnerved her. It was as if the woman had once memorized the lines and they'd stuck with her for all of these years, like a lesson drilled into an elementary school child's head. Lindsey's gut screamed that something was off, and her gut had never failed her yet.

Gripping the ornament in her closed fist, she sat in the driver's seat, weighing her options. Was there a chance Matt's father had not committed the crime? Disbelief whispered through her, her brain unable to wrap itself around the possibility. But it was as simple to question exactly what had happened that night as it was difficult to question Alessandro's guilt.

She'd always wanted the full story, had always wanted closure. Maybe now was the time to dig deeper than her uncle and his team of investigators had dug earlier.

Perhaps she'd be able to piece together those last minutes of her mother's life. The why of her murder, the where of her disappearance. Maybe Lindsey would finally be able to locate her mother's remains.

Sadness pulled at her insides.

If nothing else, she'd be happy with that one answer. Maybe once she could lay her mother to rest, she'd be able to move past the void that had haunted her life since that stormy night so many years ago.

Maybe this time, she'd find closure.

Fifteen minutes later Lindsey paced in the waiting area outside her uncle's office.

"He'll be off his call in a minute," Margaret, her uncle's secretary said. "Sit down, honey. You're making me nervous."

Nervous? That would be the day. Margaret Delaney was made of steel. She had to be to have been able to work with Frank Bell all of these years. He might be her uncle, but Lindsey knew Bell wasn't an easy man to spend a lot of time with.

Even when she'd spent the first several years following her father's death under his roof, Uncle Frank had never been able to leave his cool political edge at the office. He'd tried, but failed miserably.

Aunt Priscilla had withdrawn so frequently into the deep crevices of her mind Lindsey often felt more lonely than she would have had she stayed at her parents' house alone. As soon as she'd finished college, she'd moved back home, finding it easier to live with the ghosts of her past.

"Lindsey?" Margaret's voice broke through Lindsey's thoughts, and she lifted her gaze to meet the woman's. Margaret shot her a wink. "He's ready for you now."

She'd planned on easing into the conversation. She'd planned on gently weaving her questions into casual conversation with her uncle, but once she crossed the threshold to his office and studied him as he sorted through the paperwork on his desk, all of Lindsey's plans flew out the window.

She approached his desk and placed the ornament on top of the files beneath his nose.

"It's a little late for Christmas ornaments, don't you think?" His strong gaze studied her, and Lindsey couldn't help but notice how many more strands of gray laced their way through his thick, dark hair since he'd taken office as mayor.

"It's Mommy's."

The soft edge around his eyes hardened instantly. "Damn whoever left that license for you. What did you do? Go digging through all of her things again?"

Lindsey shook her head. "I found it at the star witness's house."

Uncle Frank's gaze narrowed and a frown line creased the skin between his eyes. "You'd better sit down and tell me what in the hell you're talking about."

Lindsey sank into one of the oversized leather chairs that faced his desk. "Lorraine Mickle."

He visibly drew in a deep breath but said nothing. Lindsey was well familiar with the move. It was one he practiced when he was trying to avoid losing his temper. Her pulse quickened. She hadn't come here to raise his ire, but she had to let him know she wasn't pleased with how he'd conducted the investigation now that she was well versed enough to scrutinize the methods that had been used.

"You based your entire case on the woman." She held up a finger. "One woman. One testimony."

"And plenty of evidence." Color played in his cheeks and Lindsey knew she was treading a fine line.

"Circumstantial."

One dark brow lifted. "Blood on the murder weapon in the man's shop?"

"Maybe it was planted. There was no body. How do you know it was the actual murder weapon?"

Her uncle stood and turned toward the window that took up most of the wall behind his desk. "You've been watching too much television, peanut."

Lindsey steeled herself. She had no intention of letting the pet name she'd clung to all of her life as a sign of her uncle's love derail her focus.

"You need to let this go," he continued. "For all you know the photocopy of your mother's license came from one of Alessandro's cronies in prison."

Lindsey squinted, not fully comprehending where he was headed with his line of thought. "You think someone's held that all of these years and just now left it as a souvenir?"

Bell turned to face her and shrugged. "I've seen stranger things." His frown deepened and he leaned against the corner of his desk. "Want to tell me why you felt compelled to talk to Lorraine Mickle?"

"I saw her name in the—" *Damn.* She'd almost told him Matt had handed her an illegal copy of the case file. She had to think fast. Her uncle's lips pressed into a flat line. "It was in an old newspaper article I found. One I must have been too young to remember."

Uncle Frank's features softened. "You're too young to be remembering it all now, too. I'd rather you let it go." He stepped toward her and planted a hand on each of her shoulders. "Move on with your life, Lindsey. Lord knows you got a lousy start, but I'd like to see you have a better go of it from here on out."

He removed his hands, turned sharply toward his desk and pressed the intercom on his phone. "Margaret, what in the hell did you do with the Prescott file?"

Lindsey pulled herself to her feet, knowing he'd effectively dismissed her while ignoring everything she'd said. She reached for the ornament and he covered it with one hand.

"Are you going to let this thing go?"

Lindsey nodded, figuring it was better to tell a little lie than to fire up the wrath of Frank Bell. He plucked the ornament from the spot where she'd placed it, fingering the sequins before he handed it back. "Didn't this used to hang in your mother's car?"

Lindsey wrapped her fingers around the ornament then lowered it gently into her purse. "It did," she said as she crossed his office toward the door. As she reached for the doorknob, she paused to turn back. "That's why I'd like to know what it was doing hanging in Lorraine Mickle's kitchen window."

She left, pulling the door shut behind her before her uncle had a chance to say another word.

MATT DID HIS BEST TO hide his surprise when Lindsey answered the door. Her long black hair had been pulled back into a severe ponytail. The style, which might have looked harsh on other women, showed off Lindsey's high cheekbones and the smooth line of her jaw.

She'd changed from her structured business attire and now wore a pair of faded blue jeans and a simple gray sweatshirt with the sleeves rolled up. Her face had been scrubbed clean of makeup and if Matt wasn't mistaken, the red rims of her eyes suggested she'd been crying.

She looked vulnerable…and human. The combination was beyond disconcerting.

He hoisted the take-out bag like a waiter working a banquet hall. "Hoagies. Hope that's all right with you."

A slight smile tugged at the corners of her mouth. "Perfect."

"That's a good look for you," he said as she took the bag from his hands.

Lindsey frowned. "The clothes?"

Matt shook his head. "The smile."

A soft blush fired in her cheeks and she turned away from him. "I'll get some plates and napkins." She pointed toward an archway as she passed. "I spread the contents of the case file on the living room floor. I thought that might be easier."

Matt stood and watched until she disappeared into the kitchen, then he settled in the living room. Sucking in a deep breath, he reminded himself of his earlier vows.

Clean slate.

Open mind.

If they played this correctly, he and Lindsey just might uncover the truth behind the night Camille Tarlington vanished.

He squatted down to get a better look at the papers and photographs spread across the wide plank floor of Lindsey's living room. He knew every word by heart, every image, every nuance of thought or clue that had been jotted down on the investigators' extensive pages of notes.

He scrubbed a hand across his face. There had to be something here—something, anything—he'd missed. All he needed was one thing to give him a direction to pursue. He knew with all of his soul his father was innocent. Just look at the facts. They were all too tidy and neat. From Lorraine Mickle's voluntary testimony to the bloody murder weapon hidden in a storage closet in his father's shop.

He shook his head. Hell. If his father had been the murderer, he'd have been too smart to be so stupid.

"Anything?" Lindsey's voice sounded close behind him and he turned his head to watch her cross the room, carrying two plates, a stack of napkins and two glasses filled with lemonade.

"Nothing I haven't read or analyzed or dreamed about a thousand times before."

She set the tray on the floor and lowered herself to a sitting position, her long legs stretched out to her side. She slid a plate in front of Matt, then reached into the bag for one of the sandwiches. As she unwrapped the deli paper, she tipped her head toward the file contents.

"I thought I knew most of what happened that night, but the more I see of this, the more I realize how sheltered my uncle kept me."

Matt turned to study her face, noting how her features tightened as her gaze lit upon the crime scene photos. The bloodied driver's seat, the smeared window, the close-up shot of the floral shears, discolored with dry blood.

He reached to slide the photos into a single pile, to tuck them away under something else, anything else. What had he been thinking? This was her mother they were talking about, not some faceless stranger.

Lindsey closed her hand over his just as he touched the first print. "It's okay."

Their gazes met and the hot, protective urge he'd experienced before burned in Matt's chest. "Is it?"

She nodded. "I can do this."

She nodded again, the move more dramatic, as if she were trying to convince herself. "I need to approach this as I'd approach any case for a client. I can detach myself and analyze the facts one at a time." She shot him what had to be the phoniest smile he'd ever seen. "I can do this."

A long while later, their sandwiches had been eaten, their glasses of lemonade had been drained and they'd talked through every shred of information at their fingertips.

"There's got to be something we're missing." Matt leaned back, stretching his arms over his head.

Lindsey let out a soft sigh, the first signs of fatigue showing in her strained, but still lovely, features. "I thought of something today when I went to see my uncle."

Alarm fired in his gut. "You went to see Bell?" His voice sounded more sharply than he'd intended and Lindsey visibly flinched.

Her pale gaze met his. "Let's get something straight right now, shall we?" Her eyes narrowed. "I didn't have to agree to help you with this. I could have pursued this all on my own, so don't think you can intimidate me with some macho attitude you've perfected for cross-examining witnesses."

A smile tugged at Matt's mouth and he did nothing to hide it, knowing the move would probably make her angrier than she already was.

"Are you laughing at me?" Daggers shot from Lindsey's glare.

Matt shook his head. "Admiring you. Now then—" he nodded toward her "—tell me what you thought of today."

She drew in a long, slow breath as if working to calm herself, all the while never softening her disarming stare. "What if the floral shears weren't the murder weapon? What if someone wanted the investigators to think they were? Smear on some blood, plant them in the closet, and there you have it. Circumstantial evidence with no body to prove anything otherwise." She shrugged.

"I thought you were dead set on the fact my father was the killer." Matt stood and began to pace tightly back and forth next to where she sat.

"I'm not saying I'm still not." Lindsey pulled herself to her feet, and once again Matt was struck by her lithe figure and her graceful movements. "I'm just very good at what I do, finding something where others find nothing. You have to admit that without the body, a different murder weapon is a very real possibility."

Matt came to a stop so close to her he felt her body heat. A long moment of silence stretched between them as he stared into her eyes. She didn't move an inch. If anything, she pulled herself taller defiantly, sending the signal he didn't intimidate her in the least.

"It's genius," he said, unable to believe he hadn't thought of it himself years before. "Why do you think there's no question like that in the notes?"

Lindsey shrugged again. "Maybe they didn't want to dig any deeper than the evidence that was available. Maybe my uncle did take the easy way out."

The magnitude of her admission wasn't lost on Matt. Lindsey Tarlington had a reputation for being brilliant yet stubborn. He knew better than to make a big deal out of the fact she'd opened her mind to the possibility of a setup.

"Well, it gives us a place to start tomorrow."

"Sounds good."

"I'll make some calls and stop by your office after my morning appointment." He crossed to the front door and hesitated, hand on the doorknob. "How deep are you willing to go with this, Lindsey?"

As he turned to face her, the determination in her pale blue eyes stopped him cold.

"I have a motto when it comes to my cases."

He raised his brows in question.

"Whatever it takes for as long as it takes," she finished.

Her words resonated in his brain as he stepped out into the cool spring night and headed toward the driveway. At long last, he might finally be close to uncovering the truth behind the night his father was framed.

UNEASE WELLED INSIDE LINDSEY as Matt stepped out into the night. Maybe she shouldn't have said anything about the possibility of another weapon. Matt's mood had visibly lifted at the mention, and even though his feelings meant nothing to her, she didn't want to give him false hope.

In her mind, Tony Alessandro remained her mother's killer, but she had to consider the fact the floral shears might not have been the murder weapon.

The blood spatter which had been documented at the scene indicated a blow to a major artery with a sharp object. That was it. A sharp object didn't automatically translate into floral shears, and if the police had been wrong about the actual murder weapon, they might have missed the clue that would have led them to Lindsey's mother's body.

Lindsey had no sooner shut the door than the phone rang.

"Hello." She answered distractedly, her mind still working over the possibility of a different murder weapon.

Silence whispered across the line and dread bubbled to life in Lindsey's belly.

"Hello?"

Her pulse quickened inexplicably. Maybe her uncle was right. Maybe she *had* been watching too much television.

Static sounded across the line. "Lindsey Tarlington." The words filtered across the line in a rasp. The caller's voice had been disguised with some sort of electronic device that not only distorted the tone but made the voice sound otherworldly. Nonhuman.

A shiver rippled down Lindsey's spine and she cast a glance toward the sidelights next to the front door, watching as the headlights on Matt's car illuminated.

"Leave it alone."

The voice spoke again before Lindsey could gather herself enough to say anything. With that, the line clicked dead.

Lindsey dropped the phone and raced for the door,

jerking it open as Matt's SUV backed out onto the street. She stepped out under the bright light above her front steps. Relief surged through her as the SUV stopped then accelerated back into the drive.

"Lindsey?" Matt's voice cut through the quiet night even as his driver's door sprang open.

She pointed back at the open front door and the cordless phone where it lay in the hall. Suddenly, embarrassment wound its way through her. She ran an agency of her own, for crying out loud. Why had she let the call rattle her so? And why had her only thought been to race for Matt?

He closed the space between them and gripped her by the shoulders. "You're pale as a ghost. What's wrong?"

She swallowed, searching for her voice, struggling to regain her composure. She had no intention of letting Matt Alessandro think she needed him. "Someone called me."

"Who?" His intent gaze bore into her own.

She shook her head. "I don't know. The voice was disguised. Distorted. He…she…it…told me to leave it alone."

Matt's dark brows lifted and he released his grip, moving past her into the house. She turned to follow his movements with her gaze, but her feet remained firmly planted on the front step.

Matt plucked the phone from the floor and rapidly punched three keys—*69, no doubt. He sighed almost instantly.

He repeated the digits as he lifted his gaze to Lindsey's. He pushed the off button then studied the phone in his hand. "Recognize it?"

Lindsey shook her head.

Matt studied the phone. "This doesn't have caller ID. Don't you think that would be smart in your line of work?"

"Never got around the getting it. I don't get many calls."

Truth was, she worked late just about every night, coming home only when she grew so tired she could no longer focus her thoughts on whatever case she was working. Some nights she never made it home at all, curling up on the sofa in the break room instead.

Regina and Tally were kind enough not to comment on the fact Lindsey often wore the same clothes in the morning she'd worn the night before. Her partners understood her hesitancy to go home to the empty house and memories of the parents who had both died too young.

Matt pulled his cell phone off of his belt. "Let me call a buddy."

He turned his back as he dialed and walked toward the kitchen, out of earshot. Lindsey was able to make out the low rumble of his voice, but nothing more. She hugged herself quickly, then stepped back into the house, pulling the outer door shut behind her.

"He's going to get back to me," Matt explained as he turned to face her. "But his initial search looks like a disposable cell phone. Probably a dead end."

"I need some hot tea." Lindsey allowed plenty of

space as she stepped past Matt, not wanting to give him the opportunity to touch her again. She hadn't liked how vulnerable and needy the move had made her feel. "Can I fix you a cup?"

He nodded. As she neared the kitchen, she sensed him following close on her heels.

"Did the caller say anything else?"

She shook her head. "Just my name."

Matt's hand pressed gently against her shoulder as she flipped on the burner beneath the kettle. She shuddered and stepped away from him.

"Sorry." A note of surprise sounded in his voice. "I didn't mean to scare you."

Lindsey turned to face him, leaning her backside against the edge of the kitchen counter. She waved a hand dismissively. "It's just been a long day."

Matt nodded. "I understand, but I need you to tell me exactly what the caller said. From start to finish."

Lindsey repeated the conversation verbatim, not that there was much to tell. When Matt questioned the caller's voice and tone, all she could do was shrug. "It was too synthesized to tell a thing. I'm sorry."

Matt stepped toward her, moving close. Too close. Lindsey thought about shifting sideways along the counter, but decided standing her ground was her best move. She couldn't help but notice the lines of concern that edged Matt's eyes or the grim set of his mouth. He was as upset about her call as she was, and that scared her more than anything else.

She'd vowed never to let herself be vulnerable. If she

remained emotionally unattached, she'd never get hurt again. The plan had worked beautifully. Until now.

Matt stepped closer still, his gaze dropping momentarily to her lips then lifting again to meet her stare. "I won't let anything happen to you. You know that, right?"

She'd known this man for little more than forty-eight hours, yet his words sent a wave of relief easing through her. "I know." The softness of her voice surprised her.

For the briefest of moments, she wondered what it would be like to let Matt Alessandro under her skin—into her life and into her heart.

He leaned toward her and she held her breath, releasing it sharply when the tea kettle squealed, announcing it had reached the boiling point.

Suddenly, reality scattered her idiotic thoughts. Matt Alessandro's father was responsible for her mother's murder, her father's depression and death and her shattered life. Tony Alessandro had taken away everything she'd had and here she stood, inches away from touching his son. Kissing his son. Or worse.

What in the hell was wrong with her?

Matt reached past her to turn off the burner, brushing against her as he did so. He shifted the kettle from one burner to another, then straightened, still touching her, shoulder to shoulder.

"Do you want me to stay with you tonight?"

Did she? "No." Lindsey stepped away then, putting plenty of distance between her and the allure of Matt Alessandro. "I'll be fine."

"What if you get another call?"

"I'll call you." She caught herself. "Or I'll call my uncle. He'll check it out."

Matt's warm gaze chilled at the mention of Frank Bell. "Maybe it's best if you didn't tell him just yet. If he finds out, he's going to do whatever he can to keep you out of this."

Leave it alone.

Matt was right. Uncle Frank would do whatever he could to keep her away from the subject of her mother's disappearance. He always had. But right now she had bigger things to worry about. Suddenly, she needed Matt out of her house, before her resolve crumbled.

"You know, I'm exhausted suddenly." She rubbed a hand across her face. "Would you mind taking a rain check on that tea?"

Matt squinted then frowned. "Sure. No problem."

He drew in a deep breath, never taking his gaze from her. Damn, but the man unnerved her.

"You'll call me if you get another call?"

Lindsey nodded quickly. "I will."

"All right." Matt crossed toward the archway to the center hall. "I'll stop by your office tomorrow. Make sure you lock up tight."

"Always," Lindsey said as he stepped outside and pulled the door shut behind him.

She flipped the deadbolt, then stood watching as the SUV eased out into the street, this time pulling away. As his taillights disappeared, Lindsey let herself sag with the emotion of the day, leaning heavily against the wall and sinking down into a sitting position.

She'd just dropped her face into her hands when the phone rang again.

Chapter Five

Matt pulled to the side of road at the end of Lindsey's street and mentally chastised himself. He'd almost kissed her, for crying out loud. If the teapot hadn't whistled, he might have let his purely male response to Lindsey Tarlington shove aside the real reason he needed her to begin with—to clear his father's name.

He didn't like leaving her when she was so obviously rattled, but putting some space between them was probably for the best.

Guilt tapped at the base of his brain. If he hadn't convinced her to revisit her mother's case, she'd probably be sound asleep or reading a good book instead of worrying about the next time her phone rang.

Matt shook his head. Not likely.

Lindsey Tarlington possessed a stubborn intensity he'd previously only seen when he looked in the mirror. Chances were, even if he hadn't shown up at her office and then at her house with the case file, she'd have launched an investigation of her own.

But the threatening phone call added to his concerns, even though it could have been a crank. Hell, for all he knew the caller could be the subject of one of her cases. After all, she did make a living by exposing people and hidden facts. He didn't like the timing just the same. He'd never been a big believer in coincidence.

A sense of alarm pulled at his gut, and his gut was rarely wrong. Chances were, whoever had made the call wanted Lindsey to leave her mother's case alone. But why? And to what lengths would the caller go to stop her?

Protectiveness washed through him. The sensation was a new one—well, new since he'd met Lindsey. There was no denying the feelings the woman inspired presented an unwanted distraction, a dimension of the situation he'd never anticipated.

Damn it all to hell.

Matt blew out a breath, flipped on the right turn signal and headed back toward Lindsey's house for the fourth time in three days. As long as she was the target of anyone's displeasure, he intended to keep a close eye on her.

Whether she wanted him to, or not.

LINDSEY STUDIED THE RINGING phone and battled the dread gnawing at her insides.

Matt was right. She needed to get caller ID. On the fourth ring she pressed Talk and held the phone to her ear, saying nothing.

After several long seconds of uncomfortable silence, her uncle's voice barked in her ear. "Lindsey? Something going on?"

She thought about twisting the truth. Thought about telling him she'd had something caught in her throat, leaving her momentarily unable to speak, but she'd never been able to lie to anyone, let alone Frank Bell.

"I got a crank call. Sorry. Thought it might be the same person calling back."

In the quiet moment that followed, she pictured her uncle pursing his lips and rubbing a hand across his face. When his words came, they were sharp and intense. "Tell me exactly what happened."

When she'd finished repeating the details of the conversation, if one could call it that, her uncle spoke with the quick confidence she'd admired throughout her life.

"I think it's unrelated to what's happened, but you can't be sure. It's probably some crackpot who heard about your mother's license and wants to play with your head."

"What if it's whoever left the copy? Or the ring?"

"There was no ring."

The annoyed edge to his voice might as well have been a slap. Lindsey opted to avoid another argument, remaining silent. She'd seen her mother's ring, whether anyone believed her or not. Check that. Matt Alessandro believed her. He was the only one who believed her.

Her insides gave a slight twist.

"Don't you think whoever left that copy wants you

to pursue the past?" Her uncle's voice refocused her attention.

She thought for a minute. He was right. "Well then, who would want me to leave it alone?"

"How about everyone. Hell, I want you to leave it alone. The story's closed. Alessandro paid for what he did."

"And then some," Lindsey mumbled, thinking about the brutal death the man had met in prison.

"What was that?"

"Nothing," she answered, thinking hard.

"Don't you let that son of his sway your emotions." His anger was palpable through the line.

Lindsey winced, realizing Matt had begun to do just that. But there was far more to her need for information. "This case will never be closed for me, Uncle Frank. Not until I find my mother and lay her to rest."

"Don't you think your aunt and I would like nothing more than that same thing? She's never been the same since she lost her sister." He inhaled sharply. "We can't always get what we want, Lindsey. That's life."

She held her tongue, waiting to hear what he'd have to say next.

"Listen." His tone grew uncharacteristically gentle. "I know how determined you are to dig up the past, but I don't want to see you relive the pain. Once was enough."

He paused and Lindsey waited again, having learned a long time ago that conversations with her uncle went much more smoothly when she kept her mouth shut instead of arguing.

"Why don't I come over tomorrow morning before work," he continued. "We'll split a pot of coffee and talk the whole thing out. Sound good?"

Lindsey's heart gave a tiny twist. The thought of securing her uncle's undivided attention had never ceased to thrill her as a teen, and her subconscious apparently still clung to the desire. "I'd like that."

"Go get some sleep."

But as she sat flipping through her mother's case file hours later, Lindsey realized she'd be lucky if she slept at all. She would not rest until she exposed the full truth behind the night her mother vanished from her life.

MATT SCRUBBED A HAND across his tired face and pulled his date book out of his briefcase. He flipped open the pages and groaned. He had two crucial depositions today and he wouldn't be doing his clients any favors showing up in his current state.

He snapped the book closed and took another swig of the coffee he'd bought hours earlier on one of his loops around Lindsey's neighborhood. He'd seen nothing out of the ordinary, but rather than going home, he'd finally pulled to a stop across the street from her drive, fighting sleep until dawn lit the morning sky with a pale pink glow.

When a light had illuminated the window to what he imagined must be her master bathroom, he realized he needed to move farther down the street. Somehow, he was fairly sure the headstrong beauty wouldn't appreciate the chivalrous intent that had gone into his watch-dog activities.

He yawned then took another swallow of the bitter coffee.

Hell, Lindsey must be just as exhausted as he was. The pale glow of her bedroom light hadn't dimmed until well after three o'clock this morning. She'd been reviewing the case file again, no doubt.

Matt grimaced. Maybe he should lift the photos the next time he saw her. There was no reason for her to relive the horror of her mother's bloodied automobile every time they reviewed the case.

Headlights flashed in his rearview mirror and he instinctively slouched in his seat. When a white, late-model Crown Victoria eased past him and turned into Lindsey's drive, he leaned across his steering wheel, being careful to keep his head low.

He whistled when Frank and Priscilla Bell crossed the house's front walk and stepped up onto the stoop. When Lindsey appeared at the door, kissed them both and ushered them inside, Matt let out a string of expletives.

What in the hell had she done? Confided in the Bells?

Matt snapped open his cell phone and punched in the number of one of his buddies down at the station. One thing was for sure. Once Frank Bell realized he and Lindsey had begun digging into the past, any remaining trace of that past was bound to disappear—namely the case's archived evidence.

Matt had every intention of beating the mighty Mayor Bell to the punch.

LINDSEY HELD BACK HER surprise when both Uncle Frank and Aunt Priscilla stood on her doorstep the next morning. Her aunt foisted a bakery box in her direction. "We brought you some sweet rolls, honey."

"Thanks." Lindsey took the box, noticing her aunt's coloring was worse than usual. If she didn't know better, she'd think the rounds of chemotherapy had been unsuccessful at beating the cancer circulating in Priscilla Bell's veins, but her aunt and uncle had promised her the lymphoma was in full remission. She did her best to fight her doubt, but they'd been feeding her half-truths to spare her feelings for as long as she could remember.

She pulled the door open wide. "Come on in. I'll get the coffee."

They settled around the distressed kitchen table, an awkward silence stretching between them as Lindsey filled the carafe of coffee then plucked an extra mug from the cabinet for her aunt. "What a great surprise to see you, Aunt Pris. How are you feeling?"

"She's fine." Uncle Frank's curt answer ended the possibility of any true discussion of her aunt's health before it could get started. "Why don't you sit down?"

Lindsey did as she was told, scraping back the chair across from where her aunt and uncle sat.

"We felt it was time to talk to you about the night your mother died."

Lindsey nodded, taking note of the fact her aunt's gaze wavered, dropping to where she clasped her hands in her lap. Lindsey poured steaming coffee into each of their mugs and nodded. "There's nothing I'd like more than to hear the full story. I know you've tried to spare me over the years, but I'm an adult now. I deserve to know whatever the two of you know."

Her uncle frowned in response while Priscilla shot him a nervous glance, then resumed her scrutiny of her hands. Lindsey had seen her aunt assume the subservient role to her uncle many times over the years, but usually only at public functions where Frank was to be the center of attention. She'd never witnessed her aunt so meek in private, when it had been just the three of them.

Lindsey reached across the table, splaying her fingers next to her aunt's mug. "Are you okay, Aunt Pris. Can I get you anything?"

Priscilla offered a weak smile and shook her head. "Just worried about you, dear. That's all. I don't want your blackouts to start again."

Lindsey winced. "They won't. I feel fine. Besides, that was a long time ago. I see enough heartache every day in my job to have thickened my skin. I can handle whatever you've got to tell me."

Her aunt blew out a soft breath. "But these are your parents we're talking about, honey. This is different."

The pace of Lindsey's heartbeat quickened. "Go ahead."

Priscilla turned to her husband. "Frank?"

Her uncle visibly steeled himself, his features stiffening into the expression he typically saved for the television cameras. "You were right to think we may have made a mistake in convicting Alessandro."

Lindsey rocked back in her chair. The reality she'd clung to for years shifted a bit with her uncle's words.

"I thought you were sure?"

Bell nodded. "We were. As sure as the evidence would allow us to be. But years later something new came to light."

Lindsey lifted her brows, not trusting her voice at that moment, afraid her disbelief would be all too evident, but then she forced one word from between her lips. "What?"

"The night your father died." Her uncle's features softened. "He left a note."

"WHAT DO YOU MEAN there's no evidence?" Matt slapped a hand against Roy Walker's desk.

Roy crooked a blond brow. "What are you going for? The Academy Award?"

Matt frowned, realizing he needed to do a better job of keeping his emotions in check. "Evidence wouldn't just disappear, would it?"

Roy shrugged. "Things happen once the boxes get archived." He ran his fingers across a photocopied sheet. "Probably got misplaced somewhere along the years. After all, it's not as if it was a cold case. We had a clean conviction and there was no chance of an appeal."

Matt drew in a long, slow breath, working to remain calm. "Yeah. It would have been pretty difficult for my dad to file an appeal once he'd been stabbed to death."

Roy winced. "Sorry, man. I wasn't thinking."

Matt tipped his chin toward the log book page Roy had copied. "Who was the last person to look at the evidence?"

A crooked grin played at the corners of Roy's mouth. "Knew you'd ask that question, and when I saw who it was, I convinced the clerk to make this copy." He held out the sheet. "Don't say I never did you any favors."

Anticipation grabbed at Matt as he reached for the paper. When his focus dropped to the last name on the sheet, his pulse roared in his ears.

The signature and printed name were clear. Frank Bell. It was the date that had been written a bit more sloppily, though still legible. Matt could barely believe his eyes. "What does that look like to you?" he asked as he handed the paper back to Roy.

Roy's grin deepened. "That, my friend, says nineteen ninety-three."

Matt frowned, excitement starting the hum in his veins. "What the hell was he doing pulling out the evidence three years after my dad had been killed?"

"I don't know." Roy shook his head. "But I'm sure you'll find out."

THE ROOM SPUN AND Lindsey gripped the edge of the table. "What kind of note?"

"A suicide note," her uncle answered. "We told no one. We thought it would be easier if you and everyone else believed he'd died in a tragic accident."

Lindsey's vision dimmed and she squeezed her eyes shut, snapping them back open quickly to avoid alarming her aunt and uncle. "What did it say?" She forced the words from her now-tight throat.

"He said he couldn't live with the pain of what he'd done to your mother, and to you."

"But that doesn't mean he killed her."

"It doesn't mean he didn't."

"So he left me? Alone?" She blinked back the moisture threatening her vision. "How could he do that?"

"Maybe he thought it was his only way out." Aunt Priscilla leaned across the table to grip Lindsey's hands in her own. "Maybe he thought you'd be better off."

"As an orphan?"

The old pain crashed around Lindsey, closing her in.

"You all right, honey?" her aunt asked. "You're awfully pale."

"You've just told me you have proof my father committed suicide and you think he might have killed my mother," Lindsey snapped. "How do you think I feel?"

She extracted her hands from her aunt's and jumped to her feet, pacing tightly back and forth across the kitchen floor.

"This is why we never wanted you to know." Her uncle had scrambled to his feet and blocked her path.

"Why?" Lindsey met his stare, able to manage only the one word.

"Because we thought it best you never realized your father may have been the one who murdered your mother."

"It's not possible." Lindsey ran a hand through her hair and pushed past her uncle. "He loved her. Loved her."

"He was only human, and humans are capable of anything, especially under emotional stress."

Jumbled thoughts flew through Lindsey's mind. "Let me see the note." She whirled to face her uncle, extending her hand.

He shook his head. "I burned it."

Disbelief washed over her. "Burned it?"

"To protect you," Aunt Priscilla piped up from where she still sat, her fingers now curled around her cup of coffee as if she was holding on for dear life.

Lindsey blew out a frustrated breath, then hugged herself. "You destroyed the note?"

Her uncle stepped close, clasping her shoulders. "The case we made was solid. Why taint your father's name?"

"What if Alessandro was innocent?" Lindsey asked.

Her uncle's gaze darkened. "Let it go."

Lindsey met his glare, but offered nothing. No words. No nod or shake of her head. They maintained the silent posture while Aunt Priscilla excused herself to use the bathroom upstairs. Lindsey could only hope the strain of the situation hadn't made her ill.

After their tense goodbyes, Lindsey sat at the foot of her staircase, cradling her head between her hands.

Let it go? No. She was suddenly more determined than ever to find out what in the hell had happened to her family seventeen years earlier.

She used the railing to pull herself to her feet, then turned and climbed the steps. It was time to rip apart her mother's studio and everything else in the attic. Piece by piece.

THE AVENGER SAT STIFFLY, ignoring the dull ache pulsating at the base of the brain.

The Avenger.

The name brought on a quick succession of chuckles that were rapidly smothered. There was work to be done.

Things had begun to get interesting.

All progress now hinged on whatever Lindsey did next.

Would she confront her past? Or would she look the other way, as she'd done most of her life?

It was interesting how a person so devoted to uncovering the truth could be so obtuse when it came to her own family history.

Oh well, the Avenger could hardly blame her. Things had been very tidy for a long time. But they were about to get messy. Very messy.

The fun was long past due.

Perhaps it was time to leave Lindsey another clue. After all, the young woman couldn't be expected to solve the puzzle all by herself, now could she?

Chapter Six

Lindsey sat in the middle of the attic, covered with dust and filled with frustration. She hadn't found a blessed thing in her mother's studio area that she hadn't found the last time she'd searched the space. Even worse, this time she'd torn into the storage boxes filled with her dad's items. She'd never expected the wave of grief the long forgotten objects had brought to life.

Her partner, Regina, had called midway through her search to see if Lindsey had forgotten her appointment with a prospective client. She had. In all her years of running Polaris, she'd never missed an intake meeting, and this had been with a particularly well-connected client—the head of a local cable dynasty.

Frustration eased through her. Her sudden obsession with her mother's death had begun to overshadow the rest of her life.

Maybe Uncle Frank and Aunt Priscilla were right. Maybe she should stop chasing ghosts and focus on moving forward.

Lindsey sucked in a deep breath and shook her head.

Not yet. Not until she'd exhausted every angle—not until she knew without a doubt exactly what had happened on that stormy night and why.

No matter how much it hurt, she needed to understand what her mother had experienced, exactly what she'd felt, and at whose hands.

Now that she knew they believed her father might have played a role, Lindsey's need for the truth was more important than ever. She had to find out what had really happened, no matter how painful that truth might be.

Regina had offered to cover for her meeting, and Lindsey had promised to be in within the hour. That had been three hours ago.

She tucked her hair behind her ears and took stock of the mess she'd made. She'd sorted and searched through five boxes of her father's belongings. The contents lay scattered across the floor in total disarray. She was so tired she could barely think, but there was one last box left to be searched. She'd never thought her father's things might provide a clue to her mother's death, but now that she knew differently, she wasn't about to stop digging.

Lindsey bolstered her resolve and pulled the carton toward her. Smaller than the boxes she'd searched previously, it was sealed with strip after strip of packing tape. Lindsey tugged until she was able to rip one corner of the box free. From there she pried open a long edge, ripping the cardboard in the process.

The contents spilled in front of her, taking her breath away.

Her father had kept what he'd called his secret drawer. As a child, Lindsey had been forbidden from peeking inside, but that dictate had only served to make her more determined to steal a glance, which she had done frequently.

The last time she'd looked had been a week before her father's accident. It had been a month before her sixteenth birthday and she'd been searching for her present. She'd found nothing.

After his death, while her other classmates had celebrated their birthday milestones with parties and sleepovers, Lindsey had marked her sweet sixteen by packing up and moving in with her uncle Frank and aunt Priscilla.

Lindsey flipped through the familiar items. Her hand stilled when it brushed across a fat manila envelope. While she recognized all of the other items as keepsakes from her father's past, she knew this particular item hadn't been in the secret drawer when she'd last looked.

Lindsey tugged at the metal clasp, breaking off one of the prongs. She lifted the flap and dumped the contents into her lap. A list of names and addresses covered a sheet of paper. A stack of invitations had grown discolored where a rubber band had kept it bound all these years.

Sweet Sixteen.

He'd been planning her party.

Lindsey swallowed down the lump in her throat, nearly choking on the rush of emotion. Her father hadn't forgotten after all.

She read a yellowed receipt for a bracelet from a jewelry store that had gone out of business during the years since her father's death.

Her father had been planning a surprise party and he'd ordered a custom bracelet. Strange behavior for a man on the verge of suicide.

Let Uncle Frank and Aunt Priscilla think her father had taken his own life out of guilt for what he'd allegedly done. Lindsey wasn't buying that theory for a second.

MATT PULLED HIS SUV INTO the parking lot of the Polaris Agency and shoved the gearshift into Park. He cut the ignition and leaned back against the seat, drawing in a deep, slow breath and holding it for a count of three before breathing out.

He needed to get a grip on his emotions.

He'd lost his temper twice during the morning's depositions, something he rarely did. If nothing else, he prided himself on being professional and cool with both his clients and his opponents.

At least today had borne out one fact he'd suspected all along. The young gang member who had been brought up on burglary charges had been framed. When the prosecution's witness had broken down and confessed to the crime, the judge had dismissed the case.

Framed.

The flavor of the day, apparently.

Matt hadn't had any time to investigate the missing evidence from Camille Tarlington's case until after his depositions were completed, but what he'd found then had sent his suspicions of Frank Bell into overdrive, clean slate or not.

Nineteen ninety-three, the year Frank had revisited the fiber samples from Camille's car and the floral shears from his father's shop, had been the year Lindsey's father died in a one-car accident.

Even more strange, the date of Bell's visit fell one week after the accident. The day after Doug Tarlington's funeral, according to the local paper's microfiche.

Never a fan of coincidence, Matt knew something had happened to make Frank Bell check the evidence. The question was what?

According to the log, Bell had signed the evidence back in no more than an hour after he'd signed the box out. So when had the disappearance taken place and how? Had he forged the log, or had the box been lifted at a later date?

Matt shoved open his driver's door and climbed out, noting Lindsey's car parked a few spaces away. The time had come to find out just what information she was holding back.

"She's on the phone," the blonde at the desk said the moment Matt cleared the threshold.

"I'll wait."

He crossed the room to the line of chairs, nodding to each of Lindsey's partners as he passed. Both studied him intently, stern expressions plastered across their faces, no doubt wondering what he'd gotten their friend into.

"Again, I apologize for being unable to attend the meeting this morning," Lindsey's crisp voice sounded from her cubicle. "I can assure you I don't make it a practice to miss client appointments, and Regina has filled me in on your interests."

Matt lowered himself into a chair as silence stretched in Lindsey's office. If she'd missed an appointment, just what had she been up to—other than meeting with her aunt and uncle? Or had the pair been the ones to keep Lindsey busy?

"Yes," Lindsey's voice interrupted his wandering mind. "I can assure you we'll do our best to locate your heir. You have my word on that. I'll call you tomorrow with an update. I expect a quick answer for you."

Matt waited for the end of the call, then stood and stepped to the opening of Lindsey's office, flashing back on the first time he'd stood in the same space, admiring the length of her shapely legs.

In a few short days he'd grown to admire far more than the woman's legs—her sharp intellect and determination for starters. But right now he had the urge to grab her shoulders and shake her, demanding to know just what the Bells and she had discussed this morning.

He drew in a slow breath, willing his muscles to relax.

"You always make such big promises to your new clients?" he asked.

Lindsey snapped her attention to him quickly,

smiling reflexively when she set eyes on him. Her response warmed his insides, but he worked to ignore his body's reaction.

"When I feel it's warranted," she answered.

Matt couldn't help but notice the smudges of exhaustion beneath her pale eyes. So he'd been right, she had been up all night.

"Come on in," she said. "Anything new?"

"Matter of fact—" he dropped into the chair next to her desk "—yes. The evidence is missing."

"What?" Lindsey's eyes grew wide and she sank back against her seat. "How is that possible?"

"From what I understand it's not uncommon. Let's face it, that box has been down there for seventeen years. A lot of things can happen."

"Like what? It seems to me the police department is in a sorry state if they can't hold on to their archives."

Color fired in her cheeks and Matt wondered what else had happened to leave Lindsey this on edge.

"For one, the archive room's been moved during that time." He shrugged. "Things get lost." He pinned her with a stare, and as usual, her gaze didn't waver. "There's also a possibility someone wanted the evidence to get lost."

"Like who?"

Matt pulled the folded sheet of paper from his jacket pocket, handing it to Lindsey. He sat quietly as she unfolded the sheet and scanned the log of those who'd signed that particular box in and out of the archive room.

Anger flashed in her eyes when she lifted her

gaze to his. "I suppose you think my uncle made the evidence disappear."

Matt gave another quick shrug. "If the shoe fits."

She squeezed her eyes shut momentarily and handed the sheet back. "It's been a very long day. Maybe you and I should start fresh tomorrow."

He couldn't ignore the strain painted across her face. Maybe it would be better to give her time to regroup. "Fair enough. Just tell me one more thing." He held the photocopy in front of her as he stood. "What's that date next to your uncle's name?"

Lindsey squinted at log entry, then visibly flinched. "May third, nineteen ninety-three."

"Any significance?"

She sighed and dragged a hand across her face. "It's one week to the day after my father was killed, if you must know. Matter of fact, we'd buried him just the day before."

"Any idea why your uncle would have chosen that particular day to review the evidence in a closed case?"

When she met his gaze this time, an emotion Matt couldn't quite peg danced in her eyes.

"No idea whatsoever," she answered.

Matt knew a dismissal when he heard one. And as he stepped back out into the parking lot, he realized just what he'd read in Lindsey's eyes.

She'd been lying.

MATT'S FACE REMAINED emblazoned in Lindsey's mind as she drove home early that evening. He'd known she hadn't been telling the truth. She may have met the man just a few days prior, but she'd grown to know him well enough to read his features.

His expression when he'd left her office had been one of disbelief.

She groaned.

If she withheld what her aunt and uncle had told her about her father's death, she'd be no better than they were. She'd be hiding evidence in order to keep things nice and tidy.

She'd never been a fan of nice and tidy. In her business, she'd learned nice and tidy typically meant some additional information lay lurking beneath what she'd seen or been told.

She and Matt Alessandro were cut from the same cloth. That much was evident from both his devotion to his father's cause and his obvious commitment to the public defender's office.

If she didn't tell him, he was bound to sniff out the information on his own. If she told Matt, the existence of the suicide note would explain her uncle's visit to the evidence archive room. But was she ready to point the finger of guilt at her own father?

While the envelope she'd found in her father's belongings suggested he hadn't been planning his death, the suicide note suggested anything but.

She sighed. If only her uncle hadn't destroyed her father's last communication.

If her father had committed the crime, Matt's father died an innocent man—the victim of a wrongful conviction—just as Matt professed.

Guilt simmered inside her. She'd devoted her whole life to the truth. How could she stop now? Matt deserved to know all of the facts. If Tony Alessandro had been innocent, his name deserved to be cleared.

Furthermore, her father's alleged suicide note did nothing to clear up the mystery of the photocopied ID, her mother's ring or her strange phone call. If anyone could help her make sense of it all, she imagined that person would be Matt.

Lindsey flipped open her cell phone and dialed Matt's cell from memory. When his voice mail clicked on instantly, she muttered under her breath then left a message.

"Matt, it's Lindsey. Listen. About today." She steeled herself then pushed through the words before she could change her mind. "I do know why my uncle might have checked the evidence on that date. We need to talk."

She disconnected as she turned her car onto her street, hoping Matt returned her call soon. Now that she'd made up her mind to tell him what she knew, she'd prefer to get it over with quickly.

As she neared her drive, a man—the same man who had left the flyer—walked down her center sidewalk. Adrenaline kicked to life in her veins.

The man stopped as she pulled into the drive, apparently waiting for her.

Lindsey climbed from the driver's seat and rounded the back of her car. "Weren't you here the other day?"

The man nodded. "Jimmy Freeman. I wanted to see if you'd thought about the flyer."

Lindsey narrowed her gaze, trying to remember exactly what the paper had said.

"Yard work. Odd jobs," he offered. "I'm mighty handy and my prices are reasonable." He swallowed, appearing a bit embarrassed at having to ask for the job. "I'm a hard worker."

Sympathy welled inside Lindsey. It was apparent the man had swallowed his pride, and it would be nice to restore her mother's massive garden to its former glory.

She pointed to the jumbled tangle of overgrown shrubs and the bald patches of dirt in between. "Do you think you could do anything with this? Make it look presentable?"

He nodded as he walked toward her. "Yes, ma'am, I could. Used to be a landscaper back in the day." He turned and headed back toward the garden, rubbing his chin as if measuring the enormity of the task he'd been given.

"Did you see an envelope?" Lindsey asked the question before she had time to think any better of the move.

Her words stopped the gentleman in his tracks. He pivoted to face her, features twisted with puzzlement. "Envelope?"

"The day you left the flyer." She thought quickly, coming up with a less suspicious version of the truth. "A friend left me an envelope and I thought you might have seen it."

She held her breath. If he said yes, she'd have a witness to the fact she hadn't imagined the object.

Freeman shook his head. "Where did your friend leave it?"

"Between the doors."

He gave another quick shake of his head. "I never opened your door, ma'am." He turned back toward the garden.

Disappointment filtered through her. He was right. The flyer had been in the storm door. The existence of the ring truly rested on her word against everyone else's.

Lindsey's disappointment morphed to shame as Freeman stooped over an especially overgrown azalea. How could she have let things get so out of hand? It was as if she'd ignored the garden as intensely as she'd ignored the reality of her family's tragic fate.

She headed for the front door but paused with her hand on the screen door handle, part of her hoping and part of her afraid to see another envelope, as if Freeman's appearance were tied to the other incident.

She pulled on the handle and let her gaze fall to the space between the outer and inner door. Empty. Just as everyone else had believed it to be the day she'd been shoved.

Lindsey refocused on Jimmy Freeman. "So what do you think?"

He smiled broadly. "I can make her shine."

Great. At least one piece of her life was about to regain some semblance of order.

They settled on a price and agreed he'd start the next morning. Lindsey had given him a business card, should he need to reach her for any reason. As she pushed open her front door, Freeman's voice sounded close behind her, sending a sliver of apprehension up her spine.

"Might I use your restroom, Ms. Tarlington?"

She turned to face him. "Please, call me Lindsey."

The older man nodded, still waiting for her reply. She knew better than to let a perfect stranger into her home, yet the man had kind eyes, one thing Lindsey had always been accurate in assessing. Plus, if he were going to be working around the yard and possibly in her house, he'd be inside alone with her sooner or later.

"Of course," she answered. "I've just got one." She gestured at the staircase. "Second door at the top of the steps."

MATT SAT IN LOU DINARDO'S office and bounced a disposable cell phone in his hand. "So a phone like this can be bought at any convenience store." He frowned. "By anyone?"

"Anyone with the money to buy one."

He'd asked Lou, the resident expert in phone traces, to run the number from Lindsey's caller. He hadn't counted on such a solidly dead end.

"I can give you the manufacturer and a list of possible retail outlets, that's it." Lou shook his head.

"Unbelievable." Matt set the phone on top of the desk.

"Progress, ain't it grand."

"It's a nightmare." Matt rubbed his eyes. "What ever happened to the good old days when anyone could trace calls?"

"You wouldn't want to put me out of a job, would you?"

"Any other ideas?" Matt studied the other man's expression. Lou was the local genius as far as phone surveillance went. Wire taps, traces, you name it. He was the man.

Lou's gaze brightened. "Voice analysis. Haven't had a good one in a long while."

"This one was distorted apparently."

The specialist rubbed his hands together. "All the better to test my skills. Think you can get a tap?"

"No problem." Matt scraped back his chair and stood. "The person on the receiving end of the call is just as interested in finding the caller as I am." At least, she had been.

He shook Lou's hand. "Appreciate your time. I'll be in touch."

Matt flipped open his phone as he stepped outside, pressing the button to restore power. He'd shut it off during dinner with his client's family—their way of thanking him for getting the burglary charges against their son dropped.

He'd left it off on the way back to the precinct, wanting a few moments of peace and quiet.

Matt had done his best to keep his anger at Lindsey under control during the evening, but the truth was the emotion had simmered just below the surface the entire evening. All he wanted now was a long, hot shower and a tall, cool beer.

He'd no sooner flipped his phone shut than it

beeped, signaling a missed message. When Matt dialed in to the message center, he frowned at the sound of Lindsey's voice. When she told him she needed to talk to him and why, the anger he'd carried all evening diminished, replaced instead by a disconcerting sense of relief.

He'd been way too upset at the thought of her lying to him. The truth was, he shouldn't care one bit, but he did.

If Lindsey came completely clean, he'd attribute her lapse in judgment to the shock of his news about the evidence. He'd give her the benefit of the doubt, even though he was probably better off staying mad at her. At least then he might find it easier to stay focused on the case.

Matt looked down at his watch—nine-fifteen.

He hoped it wasn't too late to pull a surprise visit on Lindsey, because that's exactly what he had in mind.

THE PHONE RANG JUST BEFORE nine. Lindsey snatched up the receiver, hoping it was Matt returning her call. She held back a groan when Uncle Frank launched right back into the morning's lecture.

"I wanted to make sure you've thought about what your aunt and I told you."

Lindsey held her breath for a moment, working to calm herself before she spoke. "I have, but I don't see how it's possible."

"Lindsey, it's understandable you don't want to believe your father committed suicide, but he did." His voice softened on the last words and Lindsey realized it wasn't easy for him to break this news to her after all the years of protecting her from the truth.

"I found something." The words slipped over her lips in barely more than a whisper.

Uncle Frank's voice tensed. "Like what?"

"Some of his papers. He'd planned a surprise party for my birthday. He'd ordered a bracelet for me." Her throat tightened with the emotion she'd held at bay ever since her discovery. "He wouldn't have killed himself. Not so close to my birthday."

"Desperate people do desperate things. Planning a birthday party wouldn't matter once he'd made up his mind."

Lindsey fell silent. She'd heard of similar things in other suicides. Matter of fact, she remembered her father's uncharacteristically upbeat mood the day he died. She knew that even severely depressed people often appeared happiest once they'd made the decision to take their own lives.

She decided to change tactics. "Why would you sign out the evidence from Mommy's case a week after Dad died?"

"What the hell did you do? Check up on me?" Palpable anger tinged his tone. "You're just like your mother was, stubborn as a mule."

"I'll take that as a compliment."

Lindsey pulled her spine straighter, even though her uncle couldn't see the defiant posture. Maybe he'd hear it in her voice.

"Damn it, Lindsey. Reliving all of this can't do you

any good, and it's taking a toll on your aunt. She takes off in the car for hours at a time. I have no idea where she goes. Just drives I guess." A long, low sigh filtered across the line. "She can't afford this strain at this point in her treatment."

A few moments of silence beat across the line.

"You understand how delicate your aunt's mental state is in addition to her physical state, correct?"

"I do," Lindsey answered.

"This could break her. Try to remember that."

"You never answered my question." Lindsey refused to be swayed out of sympathy for her aunt. Not now.

She had her uncle pinned in a corner. Otherwise, he wouldn't have tried to shift the focus to Aunt Pris. Frank Bell had never been one to share personal information without an ulterior motive. Never.

Uncle Frank's exasperation sounded loud and clear across the line. "I wanted to make sure we hadn't overlooked anything that might have incriminated your father."

"And had you?"

"No. The original conviction still made sense. It was perfectly justified."

Lindsey paused for a beat, letting his words sink in. "That evidence is missing."

"What? Who told you that?" Fury sounded in his tone. Lindsey was suddenly very glad they weren't having this particular conversation face-to-face.

"Matt Alessandro." She said the name softly, knowing her uncle would hit the roof. He didn't disappoint her.

"I'm warning you to stay away from him. He's a killer's son."

"Or maybe I'm a killer's daughter."

Silence stretched between them. When he finally spoke, his tone had dropped low and intent. "Leave it alone, Lindsey."

Leave it alone. The same words her caller had spoken.

"I don't know who to believe anymore, Uncle Frank. And I'm too old for you to tell me what to do."

"You'd better think very carefully about your next step before you take it, young lady. And try to remember one other thing. If one word of this leaks out, the press will have a field day with my campaign for governor. Leave the past in the past, where it belongs."

He hung up in her ear before she could say another word.

His campaign for governor.

Maybe Matt had been right all along about her uncle's true motives.

When the phone rang a moment later, she assumed her uncle had changed his mind about being done with the conversation, but only dead air greeted her when she answered the phone.

Pinpricks of dread teased the small hairs at the nape of her neck.

"Hello," she repeated.

"Leave it alone."

"Who are—"

The caller broke the connection before the words were out of her mouth.

Chapter Seven

"Who is it?" Lindsey's voice sounded sharply—too sharply—when Matt knocked on the door.

"It's Matt." He leaned close, projecting his voice through the old wooden door. "I got your call."

Lindsey snapped open the door and the striking contrast of her pale face against her black hair took him by surprise. He reached for her cheek reflexively.

"You all right?"

She took a step backward, putting distance between them. "I just got another call."

Anger and concern tangled in his gut as he crossed the foyer in two strides. "Did you get the number?"

"It's right next to the phone."

Matt snapped open his cell and dialed Lou's number, leaving the digits on his voice mail.

"Another disposable, no doubt," he muttered as he glanced down at the sequence of numbers.

"So we can't figure out who this is?" She ran her hands through her long hair. "I can't believe this."

"We can always record your calls. Maybe try voice analysis." Matt focused solely on Lindsey. A slight tinge of color had returned to her face and relief washed through him at the sight. "What did they say this time?"

"Same thing." She frowned. "Leave it alone."

He blew out a frustrated breath, determined not to jump to conclusions. "Is there any way this could be related to one of your cases instead of to our investigation?"

"I've thought of that." Lindsey shook her head. "I'm working a few birth parent searches and not much else right now, other than the long-lost heir case you heard me discussing on the phone."

"Maybe that's it. For who?"

She pressed her lips into a tight line. "Can't tell you, but it's someone big locally."

"Okay." He sucked in a deep breath. "Let's keep that one in the back of our minds. Have you pissed anyone off lately?"

A small laugh tumbled over Lindsey's lips. "Other than my uncle? Not really."

Matt narrowed his gaze but consciously stood his ground, unnerved by how much he wanted to give Lindsey a hug. "What happened?"

"It has to do with why I called you." She brushed past him as she headed for the kitchen, gesturing for him to follow. "I found something in my father's things. And my aunt and uncle showed up this morning just full of surprises."

She stopped in the archway to glance back at Matt.

He found himself momentarily distracted by the play of the kitchen light against her hair.

"Like what?" he forced himself to say.

"Coffee?" Lindsey's pale eyes widened. "This might take a while."

Lindsey set the coffeepot to brew, then turned to face Matt, taking a deep breath. He did his best to ignore the pallor of her skin and the hint of anxiousness playing across her lovely features. He'd be better off clinging to the anger he'd felt earlier than to start worrying about Lindsey's well-being.

The woman was a means to an end—a way to clear his father's name. Nothing more. Now all he had to do was remember that.

She pressed her lips together as if searching for how to say whatever it was she'd brought him here to tell him.

Matt's traitorous heart quickened its beating and he closed the space between them, unable to fight the attraction and protectiveness he felt for her. He hesitated for just a moment before he gripped her shoulders, meeting her gaze head-on.

"Whatever it is, spill it fast." He nodded encouragingly. "Just like ripping off a Band-Aid."

Lindsey made a weak effort at a smile, then spoke. "My father left a suicide note before his accident." She paused for a beat, then continued. "According to my aunt and uncle, in the note, my father hints at being responsible for my mother's death."

Matt concentrated on holding his features still. Every

muscle in his body wanted to jump for joy. This was just the break he'd been hoping for all these years. The fact Frank Bell had reexamined the evidence just after Doug Tarlington's death meant he thought he might have made a mistake.

The mighty Bell had doubt after all.

"There's more." Lindsey swallowed. "I found something in my father's things that makes me think he would have never committed suicide." She flinched. "At least not then."

She inhaled sharply again, then stepped away from Matt. "There was a time when I feared for my father." She began to pace back and forth across the kitchen. "I might have been young, but I realized my dad was never the same after the night my mom disappeared."

Sympathy tugged at Matt. He pictured the sadness that had never quite left his mother's eyes after his father's arrest and conviction, then death.

"I'm sorry," he said, meaning it, knowing his family had played no role in the heartache Lindsey and her father had experienced.

Lindsey's features softened as though his words had gotten through the protective wall she'd fixed so tightly in place.

"He'd gotten better right before he died," she continued. "My sixteenth birthday was coming and I never understood how he could have left me just then." She waved a hand dismissively. "Don't get me wrong, I always believed it was an accident." She lifted her eyes to Matt. "I still do. But I always wondered why. Why then?"

She stepped away from where she'd been pacing and crossed to the kitchen table. She slid an envelope toward Matt and tipped her chin. "I found this in the boxes from his office. It hadn't been there the week before he died. I know. I'd looked for my gift."

Matt hesitated to reach for the object. "What is it?"

"Open it."

He did as she suggested and studied the contents. Invitations. A list of names and addresses. The receipt for Lindsey's sweet sixteen gift.

He swallowed down a mixture of sympathy and disappointment.

Lindsey was right. A man who had decided on suicide wouldn't make plans for his daughter's party. At least, Matt didn't think he would. And if Doug Tarlington's death hadn't been a suicide, then perhaps he had played no role in his wife's death, leaving Matt's father the prime suspect.

"The only thing that doesn't make sense is the suicide note." Lindsey had stepped close to the table, next to Matt, and stood taking in the same collection of papers.

"Have you seen it?" Matt turned to face her, suddenly uncomfortable with the proximity of her body to his.

Lindsey shook her head. "My uncle burned it. Said he wanted to protect me…my father…our family."

"Nice of him," Matt muttered. "And convenient."

Lindsey sighed. "I know you're not a big fan of my uncle, but he's a good man."

Matt bit his tongue, knowing now was not the time to launch into a rant about Frank Bell's character.

"What do you think?" Lindsey's question was nothing more than a breath of air next to Matt's ear.

"I don't think your father killed himself." Matt straightened away from the table and turned to face Lindsey.

A wide smile broke across her face, and moisture shimmered in her eyes. Her throat worked and she blinked twice, as if wanting to hide her emotional response. She splayed one hand on Matt's chest, sending a spiral of warmth outward from her touch. "Thank you."

They stood like that for what seemed like hours, frozen in time. Then, without thinking, Matt lowered his mouth, pressing his lips to Lindsey's.

She uttered a small gasp and stepped backward away from him, her hand on her throat. "Excuse me."

As she dashed down the hall, headed for the stairs, Matt tipped back his head and squeezed his eyes shut. "Good going, Alessandro," he muttered to himself. "Way to keep your focus on the case."

LINDSEY RACED UPSTAIRS and shut the bathroom door a bit too loudly behind her. She stared into the mirror, noting her flushed cheeks and bright eyes.

What on earth had she just done?

She'd kissed him. Matt Alessandro. Tony Alessandro's son.

Well, really he'd kissed her, but she'd allowed herself to get caught up in his quiet intensity and determination. She'd let herself be drawn in to the way he wanted to help her find the truth. She'd even fallen for the genuine caring he showed for his clients.

Bottom line was she'd let him get under her skin. Slowly and surely, he'd burrowed in, moving ever so close to her heart.

Lindsey met the reflection of her eyes in the mirror.

As attractive and genuine as the man seemed, she couldn't let herself fall for him. She wouldn't. She'd had enough loss in her life already, and had no intention of setting herself up for more.

After all, when all was said and done, she and Matt might just prove the police had been right about Tony Alessandro's guilt. *That* would be a solid basis for a relationship, now wouldn't it? The victim's daughter and the murderer's son.

Lindsey shook her head and reached for the door just as Matt's voice sounded out in the hall.

"Lindsey."

She winced at the gentle tone of his voice, the palpable concern.

"I shouldn't have kissed you. I'm sorry."

The door creaked and Lindsey realized he was leaning against the other side. She pictured him with his hand over his lowered head, chestnut hair rumpled, denim shirt pulled taut across his back.

And if she hadn't already admired his obvious character, he'd explained when he arrived that he'd been at a celebratory dinner with a client's family. Imagine. She never let herself care for her clients. Oh, she cared for their situation, but she worked hard to avoid making a personal connection.

She wondered who was the wiser in their approach to their work—she or Matt?

"We got carried away by today," she answered, not believing a word she was saying. "That's all."

"Okay then," Matt's voice tightened. "I'm going to head out. I'll call you tomorrow about setting up the tap, but you call me tonight if anyone calls you again, deal?"

"Deal." Lindsey pressed her forehead to the door and wondered if his forehead pressed against the opposite side of the wood.

When she heard his footsteps on the stairs, she eased the door open and stepped into the hall, moving slowly toward the top of the steps. She glanced into her bedroom, noticing the way the moonlight streamed through her window.

Must be a full moon. How appropriate.

That's when she saw it—or rather, didn't see it.

"Matt!"

His footsteps reversed and grew closer as he climbed the staircase. He said nothing as she pointed at the empty spot where her mother's ornament had hung earlier today.

"It's gone." She shook her head, disbelief flooding through her.

"What?" He pressed one hand to her shoulder and peered past her, into her bedroom.

"My mother's ornament."

"Maybe it fell."

They rushed across the room and dropped to their

knees, searching every shadow and possible hiding place where the ornament might have landed.

Lindsey rocked back on her heels, not fully believing what had happened even as she said it. "Someone's taken my mother's ornament."

Matt slid his arm across her back, encircling her shoulders and pulling her tight against him. She didn't fight his touch, instead moving closer into the sturdy warmth of his embrace.

"We'll find out who. Don't worry. Who's been inside your house since you brought the angel home."

She drew in a deep breath. "My aunt and uncle. The man I hired. *You.*"

He let loose with a sharp laugh. "You don't think I'd take the ornament, do you?"

For one crazy, fleeting moment Lindsey wondered if he could have. After all, each piece of evidence that appeared had benefited Matt more than anyone else. Each item moved him closer to raising doubt about his father's conviction.

What if Matt had kept his father's souvenirs all these years, just waiting for the right opportunity to bring them out, to stir up the past?

"Lindsey." He gave her shoulder a little shake and she moved free of his touch.

"What?"

"I asked you a question."

She widened her eyes in response, waiting.

"Didn't you say your mother kept that ornament hanging from the rearview mirror of her car?"

"Always." She nodded.

"Was it there the last day you saw her alive?"

"It must have been." She tried to think back, remembering her mother had dropped her at school on her way to work because Lindsey had missed the bus. A shiver traced its way up her spine. "It was. I remember."

"Do you remember seeing that ornament in any of the crime scene photos?" He gripped her shoulders and turned her toward him, excitement dancing in his hazel eyes.

Lindsey shook her head and whispered, "No."

Matt smiled. "We found it." He gave her a tiny shake. "We found the first chink in the investigation. Someone took that ornament before the crime scene photos were taken."

"But why would anyone take it now?"

"Someone wanted to get it out of your sight before you realized it wasn't in those photos."

"But who?" Disbelief whispered through her. "My aunt? My uncle? The handyman?"

Matt's grin spread wide across his handsome face, excitement played across his features. "As soon as we figure that out, we're going to be one step closer to finding out who really killed your mother."

A SHORT WHILE LATER, Matt stood reluctantly at Lindsey's front door.

"Let me see what I can find on your handyman. I'll be here in the morning before he shows up for work."

Lindsey narrowed her gaze. "I'd hate to think he's involved. He seems so hon—"

"Stop." Matt interrupted her. "He showed up when you saw the ring. He showed up the day the ornament went missing." Matt ticked off the points on his fingers.

"Maybe I misplaced it."

Matt pressed a finger to her lips, warming when she didn't pull away. "Don't start doubting yourself. Pretend this is somebody else's case if you have to, but don't question a thing you feel." He dropped his hand and reached for the door, turning the lock and rattling the knob as if testing its strength. "What do you know about him?"

"His name's Jimmy Freeman. Said he needed the work." She squeezed her eyes shut, searching her brain for anything else he might have said. "He used to be a landscaper." She refocused on Matt. "And he was on foot. Maybe he's staying close by."

Matt frowned. "It's not much, but it's a start." He gave the doorknob another rattle. "This thing needs to be replaced. You've got an alarm system, right?"

She shook her head. "Never needed one."

"Deadbolt? Chain?"

"This is Haddontowne." She lifted his hand from the doorknob and gave it a squeeze before urging him across the threshold. "Most of us don't even lock our doors."

Matt turned to face her, uncomfortably aware of the tension sizzling between them. Lindsey tucked her hair behind both ears, and he flashed back on the feel of her lips beneath his.

"You sure you'll be all right?" The words sounded husky, even to his own ears.

Lindsey nodded. "I'm a big girl."

"Call me if you need anything. Anytime."

She nodded again and Matt turned, taking her front steps two at a time on his way to the SUV.

"Hey, Matt."

Her voice stopped him in his tracks. He pivoted to focus on where she stood.

A warm smile curled the corners of her mouth. "Go home and get some sleep." She pointed across the street. "No more guard duty."

So she'd spotted him after all. "So much for my stealth stake-out." He grinned, enjoying the comfortable banter between them.

Lindsey gave a quick wave, stepped back inside and shut the door.

As he drove away, Matt fought the urge to circle back, whether she saw him or not. Chances were, though, she'd be fine for tonight. Both the ornament thief and her anonymous caller were probably done for the night.

But as he ran their possible identities through his brain, Matt fervently hoped Lindsey was among those Haddontowne residents who *did* lock their doors.

After all, the case was becoming more and more compelling for the argument that her mother's murderer was still on the loose.

FOR A LONG TIME AFTER Matt left, Lindsey sat at the foot of the steps running through every possible scenario for where the ornament might be.

After a thorough search of the kitchen and center hall, both places she might have set down the ornament without taking it upstairs, she went up to bed. Her lack of sleep the night before was catching up. A numbing exhaustion seeped deep into her bones.

Before she climbed into bed, she lay flat on her belly and scanned the floor beneath her nightstand and bed, on the off chance she and Matt had missed spotting the fallen ornament.

Nothing.

But what if she *was* wrong. What if she'd never hung the ornament?

Lindsey shook her head, taking Matt's advice to erase her doubt. She remembered specifically hanging the ornament in that particular window so that she could be reminded of her mother—and her case— upon waking each day.

Someone had taken the sequined angel. And with Matt's help, she'd find out exactly who, and why.

Her gut told her they were getting closer, maybe too close for whoever was involved, but she wasn't about to stop now.

No way.

Lindsey climbed under the covers and clicked off the bedside lamp, succumbing instantly to her fatigue.

She wasn't sure how long she'd been asleep when she woke sharply from a dream, knowing instantly she wasn't alone in the house.

The distinctive creak of a floorboard in the down- stairs center hall brought her fully awake. Fear clutched at her throat, and she sat bolt upright in bed, reaching for the nightstand lamp. At the last moment, she hesitated, her fingertips a fraction of an inch from the switch.

Surely she was imagining things—overreacting. After all, the past few days had left her beyond tired and strained.

The creak sounded again, sending the small hairs at the back of Lindsey's neck prickling to attention. Not wanting to call attention to herself, she left the lamp dark. She lowered her feet to the cool floor and padded silently across to the door. With a skill resulting from years of practice, she eased the bedroom door shut, quietly turning the antique lock as she did so.

Her heart pounded so loudly against her ribs she was sure whoever lurked downstairs must hear her— and her fear.

She grabbed the bedroom extension, breathing a sigh of relief when a strong dial tone sounded in her ear.

Then Lindsey held her breath and dialed 9-1-1, praying the police would get to her before whoever was busily exploring the downstairs decided to check out the bedrooms.

Chapter Eight

Matt had gone straight to the county building after leaving Lindsey's house. The public defender's office had invested in several subscriptions to online databases, and even though it was a long shot, with what little information Lindsey had given him, he might have a chance of learning something about Jimmy Freeman.

Lindsey had approximated the man's age as mid-sixties. Based on the fact he'd walked to Lindsey's house and was actively looking for work, Matt guessed he must live nearby. Yet he must live in affordable housing, which didn't make a whole lot of sense. That particular section of Haddontowne was far from cheap.

Search after search failed to turn up any potential matches.

Matt tried an employment search. A driver's license search. A credit search.

Nothing.

Suddenly, an idea popped into his brain that might

explain the entire scenario. Why hadn't he seen it sooner?

A personal history this blank usually meant only one thing. The man had been in jail for a very long time.

Matt pulled up the criminal history database and plugged in the name. He hit on three convictions for three different James Freemans. One of them, however, matched the age approximation to a tee.

Matt whistled.

First degree murder.

"Son of a—"

He was just about to search for the list of jails where Freeman had served time, when his cell rang.

"Thought you'd want to know what just came over the scanner." He recognized the voice of a buddy in the defender's office immediately.

"What?"

"9-1-1. Possible intruder."

Dread pooled in the pit of Matt's stomach.

"Where?"

"Address belongs to Bell's niece. Thought you'd want to—"

Matt slammed down the phone, plucked his keys off the top of his desk, and ran—filled with a sense of urgency like none he'd ever known.

He never should have left her alone. Not in that house. Not with those flimsy locks.

Incredulity hit him like a slap in the face. What a fool he'd been. He should have stayed just in case, no matter what Lindsey had said.

Hell, they could have pulled Freeman's information in the morning at Lindsey's office. After all, investigations were her business.

From this point on, he was sticking to the woman like glue, no matter how loudly she protested.

Matt had his SUV in gear a fraction of a second after the ignition caught, shoving the truck into reverse and squealing out of his parking space.

He didn't slow for the exit, instead careening out onto the now deserted downtown street. Matt had one thought and one thought only—getting to Lindsey as fast as he could.

The fear welling inside him overwhelmed his senses. Perhaps he could attribute his emotional state to Lindsey's earlier pallor, her fatigue, the strain she'd been under.

He might try to excuse the depth of his feelings as concern for the woman, but he'd be lying.

The unmistakable tingle of adrenaline pumping through his veins meant only one thing. His efforts to keep Lindsey Tarlington out from under his skin had failed.

Her warmth and intellect, her smile and her anger— all of it, every single facet of her person—had grown to mean more to him than he cared to admit.

Matt pressed the accelerator flat to the floor and ran a red light, racing as fast as he could toward Lindsey's supposedly safe, suburban neighborhood.

He realized that if any harm had come to her, he might be capable of murder himself. The sobering thought rocked him to the core.

Had his mild-mannered father once felt the same way?

Had Tony Alessandro been involved with Camille Tarlington after all? If they'd quarreled as Lorraine Mickle claimed, there was no telling what his father might have done in a fit of rage—although rage had been a rare emotion for the elder Alessandro.

Matt blew out a frustrated breath, wishing like hell he'd gone for a vehicle with a bigger engine. As he made the turn onto Lindsey's street, myriad flashing, blazing lights greeted him.

His stomach pitched sideways.

At that moment he cared far more about whether or not Lindsey was safe than he did about clearing his father's name.

The realization terrified him—almost as much as his fear he might be too late.

"YOU KNOW THIS IS the second false alarm you've called in to the precinct, Lindsey."

Indignation simmered inside her, threatening to bubble out in a string of expletives Lindsey was quite sure her uncle had never heard her use.

"I know what I heard." She hugged herself, suddenly wishing she were still in her jeans and sweater and not standing as the object of Frank Bell's scornful gaze wearing only her nightgown and robe.

"Really?"

He smirked and Lindsey's indignation shifted into anger.

"I'm not an idiot, Uncle Frank. I know when an intruder is in my own home."

He held up both hands. "Let's not get carried away, peanut."

"Don't you 'peanut' me. How can you not believe me?"

"Tell you what." He patted her shoulder. "I'll believe you if you want me to, but as long as there is no sign of forced entry and nothing out of place, there's not much to go on."

Lindsey pulled herself up taller. "What about fingerprints? Maybe we should call out the crime scene unit?"

Her uncle's only response was a glare full of disdain.

Annoyance shifted inside her. The last thing she needed at this particular moment was his condescension.

Lindsey hoisted her chin in his direction. "How'd you get here so fast?"

"Don't you think someone's going to call the mayor when there's a report of an intruder at his niece's house?"

She considered his statement for a second, realizing it made perfect sense. "You could have just called. I wouldn't want to draw any negative attention to your precious campaign."

Her uncle stepped close, hooking his fingers beneath her chin, something he hadn't done since she was a small child. "You don't have to be so tough all the time. Let your family worry about you now and then."

"All right," she answered softly.

The responding officer nodded toward Uncle Frank.

"Be right back," he said as he dropped his touch and crossed the living room to where the young man stood.

They spoke quietly, so quietly Lindsey couldn't pick up a single word. After a few moments, the officer tipped his hat to her, turned and left. She was alone with the mighty Mayor Bell, and no doubt in for another lecture.

He closed the space between them and looked down at her. "Everything checks out. Outside and in. You've got your imagination working overtime rehashing this whole thing with your mother."

"I know what I heard," she ground out between clenched teeth.

"Go get some sleep. You'll realize in the morning you need to drop this."

Lindsey drew in a long, slow breath, hoping he'd take her silence as a hint to leave. Uncle Frank fished in his shirt pocket, then held out his hand to her. A small, blue capsule sat squarely in his palm.

"What's that?" Disbelief rippled through her.

"One of your aunt's sleeping pills." He thrust his hand nearer still. "Take it. Some solid rest will do you good."

Lindsey shook her head, frowning. "I don't take pills. Especially pills that dull my senses."

Uncle Frank snagged one of her hands and pressed the capsule into her palm. "Keep it then. In case you change your mind." He stepped close and planted a quick kiss on her forehead. "I'll call you tomorrow to see how you are."

He turned before she could utter another word of

protest, crossing the living room with only a few, bold strides. The disbelief and anger in his voice were unmistakable when he reached the front door.

"What in the hell are you doing here? Haven't you already caused enough trouble for my niece?"

"WHERE IS SHE?" MATT leaned to look around Bell, in no mood to enter into a verbal sparring match.

When he spotted Lindsey standing in the living room, apparently unscathed, he swallowed. Hard.

"She doesn't want to see you," Bell barked out, blocking Matt's path.

"Yes." The serious note in Lindsey's voice was unmistakable. "I do."

She stepped closer to where they stood and hugged herself. Fury shimmered in Bell's gaze, and he glared at Matt before turning back toward Lindsey. "Remember what I said."

She merely nodded.

Bell slammed the door on his way out, and Lindsey launched herself into Matt's arms and buried her face against his neck before he could say another word.

A mixture of surprise and relief ignited inside him. "Are you okay?" he spoke softly into her hair.

She nodded, saying nothing.

"I shouldn't have left you. I'm sorry."

Lindsey pushed away, staring him in the eye. "The one time you listen to me, I'm wrong."

He smiled and pressed his palm to her cheek. "What happened?"

She gave a quick shrug. "I heard someone. I know I did. But there was no sign of anything…or anyone."

"Someone with a key?"

Her pale eyes widened, flashing with surprise. "Only my family has a key. Matt, you can't honestly think—"

Matt lowered his mouth to hers before she could say another word, tasting more deeply than he had earlier tonight. To his relief, Lindsey wrapped her arms around his neck, twining her fingers into his hair. Her lips opened beneath his, and his tongue tangled with hers.

Desire flared inside him, coiling into a tight knot of need. He broke their embrace, holding her at arm's length.

Lindsey's cheeks had flushed to a deep rose.

Matt felt heat fire in his own face, yet he searched for the right words, not wanting to end this moment, but needing to know exactly what had happened. "I got a little carried away," he offered as a means of explanation. "I was so…frantic on the way over."

A soft smile played at the corners of Lindsey's mouth. "I don't quite know what to make of you, Matt Alessandro."

He wrapped an arm around her shoulders and guided her back toward the living room, tucking her tightly against his side. "Let's worry about that later. Right now, I want you to tell me exactly what happened. Step-by-step. Moment by moment. Even things that might not seem important. Okay?"

"Okay," Lindsey answered softly.

On the sofa, Lindsey snuggled beneath Matt's arm while she held his other hand. Their fingers interlaced, moving slowly against each other, heat building between them—unmistakable, scorching heat—from something so simple as the touch of their hands.

Matt thought about retracting his touch from Lindsey's to concentrate fully on her every word, but the moment she'd launched herself into his arms and opened herself to his kiss, they'd crossed over from investigative partners to man and woman, each hungry for the other. The way he saw it, there was no turning back now.

When Lindsey was done explaining how the police had found nothing out of the ordinary, she released a tired breath. "I swear it's a conspiracy. The whole police department thinks I'm paranoid."

Matt gave her hand a squeeze. "Even if they do, I believe you. I know you saw your mother's ring and if you say someone was in this house tonight, then someone was in this house tonight." He narrowed his gaze. "You're an intelligent woman. People know you wouldn't make this stuff up."

"Maybe so." Lindsey lifted her pale gaze to Matt's. "If whoever was in this house tonight didn't leave anything, or take anything, why were they here?"

A shadow of fear passed over her beautiful features and concern churned in Matt's stomach. "You're not staying here alone anymore. I'll sleep right here on the sofa, or you can come back to my house with me, but no more being by yourself without me. Understood?"

"I really can take care of myself."

"So you keep telling me."

The familiar flash of life sparked in Lindsey's eyes and Matt smiled. "Knew that would get a rise out of you."

"I don't need you to protect me. You've got your own life."

Silence beat between them, and no noise sounded from outside. Mayor Bell and his troops must have gone home for the night. Why wouldn't the man have insisted on a more thorough processing of the scene? Whatever the reason, Matt knew one thing. He wasn't going anywhere.

"What if I wanted to protect you? What if you've suddenly become a very real part of my life?"

Lindsey swallowed and leaned away momentarily. "You've only known me for a few days."

"Sometimes that's all it takes."

He kissed her then, more forcefully than before, lowering her down onto the length of the sofa. She shifted beneath him, deepening the kiss and brushing one long, bare leg against his jeans.

A moan sounded from somewhere deep inside him, and Matt knew he was a goner. What little restraint he'd had left failed him completely. He lay alongside Lindsey, pressing the length of his body against hers as he traced one hand over each of her luscious curves.

When his thumb brushed against the swell of her un-encumbered breast beneath her robe and nightgown, Lindsey broke their kiss, then pressed her lips to the line of his jaw.

If Matt didn't know better, he'd swear he was about

to explode. The feel of her soft lips on his face was almost more than he could take. He ran his hand down over the curve of her waist and hip, down to the hem of her nightgown. Hooking the edge with one finger, he slid the silky material slowly up and over her thigh, trailing his hand lightly against her skin as he did so.

Lindsey shifted her kisses to his neck and Matt was able to admire the silky expanse of her now-exposed legs. Unable to take things this slowly, he turned and kissed her. Hard. He eased her back down onto the sofa and lowered himself on top of her.

Her body was warm and welcoming beneath his as he pressed his hard length into her stomach. Lindsey opened her legs, cradling him between her thighs.

Matt trailed kisses down to the hollow at the base of her throat, then lower still, teasing at the lacy edge of her nightgown where her cleavage began.

He snaked his tongue out ever so slightly, tasting the satiny skin.

Lindsey writhed beneath him.

"You're beautiful," he whispered against her skin, and Lindsey stilled.

Matt raised himself slightly, loosening the tie on her robe, then folding back the soft material to expose her nightgown. The soft fabric had bunched above her hips and he shifted to plant a kiss on her belly, smiling when she arched into his touch.

He slid a finger along the elastic edge of her panties, teasing the fabric lower and lower until he was able to touch the moist heat building between her legs.

Lindsey bucked ever so slightly against him, and he lowered his mouth to the spot, tasting her sweetness and tracing his tongue against her tender flesh.

She inhaled sharply and cradled his head between her hands, running her fingers through his hair.

Matt cupped his palms over her hips, teasing her with his tongue, enjoying her every shudder and moan, losing himself in the sensation of giving her pleasure. When her orgasm broke he kissed her gently, then cradled her in his arms, whispering softly against her hair.

"Are you all right?"

"Mmm-hmm. It's just been a long time."

Matt nibbled at the soft skin beneath her ear, relishing the fact she'd opened herself to him.

"Matt?"

Nervousness flickered through him at her tone, and for a fleeting moment he feared she'd let her head overrule her heart. "What?"

She pushed away from him, looking deeply into his eyes. "Would you check the door before we do what I think we're about to do?"

He pushed himself up off the sofa in one swift move. "I'll be right back."

A LONG WHILE LATER, Lindsey slipped into her robe and stared down at Matt's sleeping form. Was she insane?

Maybe.

She'd just made love with the son of the man who

many believed had killed her mother. The thing was, Lindsey couldn't quite wrap her mind around Tony Alessandro's guilt any longer.

How could any man of Matt's caliber be the son of a murderer? It wasn't possible.

She kneeled beside him and ran a finger along the line of his jaw. It wasn't just the way Matt made her feel that made him so attractive, though she had to admit the sex had been mind-numbing.

No.

The emotions she experienced whenever she was with him went far deeper than lust.

Her heart twisted inside her chest.

After her parents had died, she'd vowed never to love another, yet here she sat, falling undeniably for this man. Was it love? It was too early to know for sure, but the moment he'd shown up at her front door tonight, she'd realized she no longer felt alone.

And alone was something she'd felt for a very long time.

"You okay?" Matt's sleepy gaze studied her.

She grinned. "Just admiring you." She tipped her head toward the staircase. "How about we go up to bed? Neither one of us will be able to move if we sleep on this sofa."

Matt stood and plucked his jeans from the floor, slipping into them a bit stiffly. He zipped the fly, but left the button undone.

Lindsey's mouth went dry.

"Trust me," he winked. "I'm not going to be able

to move tomorrow and it's got nothing to do with the sofa."

He wrapped one arm around her, splaying his fingers against the small of her back. Heat seared through her robe, and he pulled her tightly against him, lowering his mouth to hers. With just one kiss, he erased every one of her lingering doubts.

As they turned and headed toward the hall, Lindsey spotted the blue capsule her uncle had given her. Apparently it had fallen out of the pocket of her robe during their undressing. She bent to pick it up then set it down on an end table.

Matt hoisted his chin. "What's that?"

She cringed. "Uncle Frank thought I might need help sleeping, but somehow I'm feeling incredibly relaxed."

Just then, an unfamiliar object caught her eye— something out of place, tucked into the corner of a collage of family photos. Lindsey squinted at the frame, stepping close. When she brushed her fingers across the long forgotten object, she gasped.

Matt was beside her in a flash. "What's wrong?"

Lindsey gently removed the old photo from the edge of the frame where someone had carefully placed it. "We missed this when the police were here."

"What is it?"

Lindsey stared down into the face—her own face. "My first grade picture. It was my mother's favorite. I'd just lost my front teeth."

Confusion played across Matt's face. "It wasn't there before?"

She gave a slight shake of her head.

"Then where did it come from?"

"My mother's wallet."

Lindsey raised her gaze to Matt's, not fighting the tears welling in her eyes. "Someone's got my mother's wallet. Who?"

He bundled her into his arms, pressing a soft kiss against her hair. "I don't know, sweetheart, but we're going to find out."

He pushed her out to arm's length. "Together," he added.

But Lindsey couldn't tear her focus away from the photo. In it, her gap-toothed grin lit up her face. Her bangs had apparently been cut just before the shot had been taken. Her mother never had been able to make them straight, and this haircut was no different.

Black hair zigzagged across her forehead. But, the one feature of the photo that grabbed at Lindsey's heart more than anything else was the naive joy in her six-year-old face. What she wouldn't give to go back to that moment, to a time years before tragedy would alter her life forever.

As she continued to stare at the photo, Lindsey felt close to her mother for the first time in a long time, yet the chasm of seventeen years stung more deeply than it had ever stung before.

The blissful calm she had felt after making love with Matt slipped away and her tension returned, digging its way back into her every muscle and nerve ending.

For a few hours, she'd forgotten all about her mother

and Matt's father. She'd forgotten about tracking down whoever had left the photocopy and the ring. She'd forgotten about tapping her phone and finding out why Lorraine Mickle had had her mother's treasured ornament.

As Lindsey stood staring down at the tattered photograph, reality came rushing back, and she realized the only way to find the truth was to keep her guard up—whether that meant pushing Matt away emotionally or not.

Her past had crashed into her present like a freight train, and she'd let nothing—and no one—shift her focus away from uncovering the truth.

Chapter Nine

Matt woke from his dream with a start. In it, Lindsey had been trapped in a burning house and he'd been the only hope to save her. Her screams still rang in his ears even now that he'd wrenched himself awake to get away from the nightmare.

Ever since his father's conviction, Matt's reoccurring dream had been one in which he couldn't move his feet. He'd witness some horrific event, but he'd be unable to help.

Until today, those events had centered on people and places related to work. Clients. Prosecutors. Judges. But today's dream was different.

Today's dream centered on Lindsey.

Matt ran a hand up into his hair and realized he'd been sweating. He closed his eyes and drew in a deep breath, working to slow the frantic beating of his heart. The flames of the burning house blazed on the back of his eyelids and he quickly snapped them open.

His gaze fell to Lindsey's side of the bed and her pillow—her empty pillow.

They'd gone up to her bedroom after the discovery of the photo, but neither had slept right away. Matt had cradled Lindsey against him, but her body had stiffened. Eventually she'd rolled away from his embrace, feigning sleep.

He hadn't bought the act, knowing she'd put her emotional walls back in place, disregarding the intimacy they'd shared.

Matt swallowed down his disappointment. Could he blame her? The living hell of her past was being paraded before her, one clue at a time.

The question that had hung in the air since the appearance of the first photocopy hung there still. Who possessed Camille Tarlington's personal effects, and how had he or she gotten them?

The doorbell rang and Matt squinted at the clock. Seven-thirty. Damn. Once he'd fallen asleep, he'd really gone out. He dragged a hand across his eyes and swung his legs over the side of the bed, wondering if Lindsey had gotten any sleep at all.

Today was bound to be long and busy. If they had any luck at all, they were about to get a whole lot closer to the truth.

THE DOORBELL RANG JUST as Lindsey tested the last floorboard in her mother's studio.

Jimmy Freeman.

She must have lost track of the time.

She stood and brushed the dust from her sweatpants, moving quickly toward the attic steps while fighting back her disappointment at finding no secret hiding places in the attic.

Once Matt's breathing had become even and deep during the night, she'd slipped out of bed, pulled on a pair of old sweats and headed for the attic. Unable to sleep, and afraid of what she'd dream if she did, she'd decided to look for hidden pockets beneath the attic floor.

Maybe she'd watched too many old movies, but she'd figured one last search might work. Perhaps she was growing desperate, but she needed something—anything—to give her the upper hand against whoever it was that was trying to manipulate her every move.

Truth be told, she'd also needed to move away from Matt. As much as her head wanted to ignore the fact they'd made love, her heart had begged her to turn into his touch, hiding beneath the protective warmth of his embrace.

She'd never needed anyone's protection, and she didn't plan to start doing so now. She was strong and independent. Always had been and always would be.

The doorbell rang again as she neared the bottom of the stairway. When she peered through the narrow window framing the front door, Jimmy stood stiffly on the top step, his expression fixed with what she read as nervousness.

Lindsey took a deep breath then pulled open the

inner door, determined to find out if the man was responsible for her missing ornament.

"Good morning, Ms. Tarlington."

Jimmy's smile looked genuine enough, Lindsey thought. She studied his body posture, not noticing any sign of aggression or lying.

He frowned. "You all right this morning?"

Lindsey pursed her lips. "Not really. Had a lousy night's sleep." She crooked a brow. "Do you know anything about why, Mr. Freeman?"

He looked worried now, and Lindsey wondered if she'd hit a nerve.

"No, ma'am. Did something happen?"

Lindsey nodded and narrowed her gaze. "So you're sure you don't know a thing about what went on here last night?"

His brows puckered together. "No, ma'am. I'm sorry if you've got troubles."

Lindsey blew out a frustrated breath and tried to think of how to get Freeman to admit his involvement. After all, he was her prime suspect at this point. Maybe if she provided him with a few facts, she could trick him into saying something about what had happened.

"I recently found an ornament that had belonged to my mother." She hugged herself then dropped her arms, not wanting to show any sign of insecurity. "I made it in elementary school for her. A sequined angel. Have you ever seen such a thing?"

Jimmy squinted, obviously confused by the conversation. "No, ma'am."

"I discovered it missing last night," Lindsey said. "Apparently, someone took it. Someone who's been in my home." She drew out the last three words, driving her point home.

Jimmy paled, and Lindsey thought perhaps his facade might start to crack. Her frustration grew when he said nothing.

Lindsey leaned toward him, pinning him with her gaze. "Did you take that ornament, Mr. Freeman?"

He swallowed visibly and shook his head. "No, ma'am. I'm not a thief."

"But you are a murderer. Aren't you?"

The deep rumble of Matt's voice sounded just behind Lindsey, sending a shiver up her spine.

She'd been so engrossed in questioning Jimmy she hadn't heard Matt come down the stairs. Her heart jumped at his words, and she spun to face him. "What are you talking about?"

"I served my time," Jimmy said.

"The question is where?" Matt stepped next to Lindsey, planting one hand on the doorjamb and the other on her back.

Lindsey could barely believe her ears. Freeman was an ex-con? A convicted murderer?

"Graterford," Jimmy answered.

Lindsey's throat tightened and a rush of blood buzzed in her ears. *Graterford*—where Tony Alessandro had been incarcerated and killed.

A spike of adrenaline overcame the exhaustion in her veins and she whirled on Jimmy.

"Did you know Tony Alessandro? Did he give you these things to bring to me? Why? To haunt me? To bring it all back?"

Jimmy's eyes had gone huge. Matt hooked a hand through Lindsey's arm, squeezing tight. She tried to jerk free of his grasp, but had no luck.

At that particular moment, she wanted nothing to do with him. He'd known about Freeman's conviction and yet he hadn't said a word. He'd withheld information, probably because that information might very well point the finger of guilt squarely back at his father.

Jimmy took a step backward, dropping down one step. "I don't know a thing about what you're saying, Ms. Tarlington. I don't."

"You never knew my father?" Matt spoke the words in a hesitant mix of hope and dread. "Tony Alessandro? He died there about sixteen years ago."

Part of him craved contact with anyone who had known his father—anyone who could fill in the gaps of those last six months of his life. Matt would take whatever memories of his dad Freeman could provide.

Lindsey squirmed next to him, and he tightened his grip on her arm. He didn't want to hurt her, but knew she'd probably shift her anger from Freeman to him the second he let her loose.

He should have told her about Freeman's conviction last night, but he hadn't wanted to upset her any more than she already had been by the evening's events. He'd intended to tell her this morning before Freeman's arrival, but oversleeping had dashed that plan.

Jimmy shook his head slowly from side to side. "I never knew Tony Alessandro, I'm sorry." He nodded quickly. "I do remember the stabbing." The set of his mouth grew grim. "Prison's a terrible place to be, let alone to die."

Pain squeezed at Matt's chest, but he fought it down, focusing instead on reading Freeman's expression for any sign of lying. He saw none.

"Then why are you here?" Lindsey asked, her voice tighter and higher than usual.

"I need the job, ma'am. That's all." Jimmy turned to leave. "I can see I've worn out my welcome. I'll go."

"Stop." Lindsey broke free of Matt's grip and dashed down the stairs after Freeman. "I need to know why you singled me out."

The older man turned to face her, a sadness framing his watery eyes.

"Admit it," Lindsey persisted. "I saw you with flyers, but I never saw you at any door but mine. And you came back. You persisted in getting close to me. Why?"

"I saw you in the paper."

Matt's pulse quickened. Was the man a stalker?

Freeman's features tensed and Matt mentally prepared himself to jump between the man and Lindsey if he should make a move.

Freeman's throat worked. "I wanted to hire you to help me." He shook his head. "I don't have much money, so I needed the job to pay you."

Moisture glimmered in the older man's eyes and Matt frowned. Was he telling the truth?

"Hire me for what?"

Lindsey had taken a step closer to Freeman and Matt realized she'd begun to soften to the man's story.

"I know you find people." Jimmy shrugged. "I need to find someone."

Lindsey's shoulders sagged. "Why didn't you just tell me that from the beginning?"

Freeman's features crumpled. "I was ashamed."

Lindsey hugged herself and Matt stepped down next to her, standing eye to eye with Freeman.

"Who do you want to find?" he asked.

"The wife of the man I killed." Freeman spoke the words without hesitation, unlike the typical convict who professed innocence above all else.

Matt thought of his father's professions of innocence and winced.

"Why did you kill her husband?" Lindsey asked.

Jimmy met her gaze squarely, holding his chin high. "He was going to beat her to death. I did what I had to do."

"He abused her?" Matt asked.

"Yes."

"So why the long sentence?"

"Because she vanished. She didn't stick around to testify on my behalf. They put me away for premeditated murder." He hoisted his chin even higher. "I'm not sorry for what I did. The man was evil."

If Freeman was telling the truth, Matt wished he'd been around to defend him. While murder was never justified, in this case, it sounded as if Freeman's charges might have been decreased to lower his time served.

"Well then, I guess you're ready to get to work?"

Lindsey's voice sliced through Matt's thoughts, filling him with disbelief. He turned to study her expression.

"Can I bring you some coffee, Jimmy?" she asked.

"No, ma'am." Surprise flickered across Freeman's features, and Matt realized the older man was as stunned by Lindsey's change of heart as he was.

"Please, call me Lindsey. And I'll leave the door unlocked in case you need anything. You know where the bathroom is."

Jimmy tipped his chin to her. "Yes, ma—Lindsey."

She smiled. "I'm sorry for your troubles, Jimmy. Maybe a little later on we can talk about this woman you want to find."

"You should know—" Jimmy put a hand on his chest "—I mean her no harm. I'm not mad at her for running away. I just want to know she's okay. I don't even want to talk to her, though if she wanted to talk to me, that would be fine." He gave a weak smile. "I loved her once."

"And probably saved her life," Lindsey said. "I'll get my mother's old gardening tools from the shed, and you let me know if you need anything else, you hear?"

"Yes, ma'am."

Matt caught up to her just inside the door. "You're still going to let him work here?"

She spun on him, daggers flashing in her pale eyes. "At least *he* didn't lie to me."

Matt flinched. "I was going to tell you this morning.

I didn't think you needed anything else to worry about last night."

"What's the matter? Were you afraid he *did* know your dad? That maybe he'd corroborate your father's guilt?"

Matt stepped back as if she'd slapped him.

Lindsey squeezed her eyes shut then looked up at the ceiling. "I'm sorry," she said softly. "It's just another dead end, that's all." She lowered her gaze to his, frustration etched across her face. "Sorry."

Matt pulled her into his arms and kissed her cheek. "It's okay." He stepped back, dropping his touch. "Did you sleep at all?"

"No." She blew out a sigh. "I searched the attic looking for a loose floorboard."

Matt squinted at her. "Why?"

"Because my gut tells me I'm missing something. Don't you think that if your father and my mother were having an affair there'd be some sort of physical evidence?"

"Haven't we had this conversation?" Matt asked.

"Well, don't you?" Color flared in her cheeks.

Matt shrugged. "I never believed they were having an affair. I thought you didn't, either?"

Lindsey's throat worked. "I don't know what I believe anymore."

Matt's cell phone vibrated against his waist and he pulled it from his belt to read the incoming number. Work.

"I have to take this."

Lindsey nodded. "I'll go make some coffee."

A few moments later, he stepped into the kitchen, concern washing through him when he spotted Lindsey sitting on the floor, slumped against a cabinet.

She looked up when the floor creaked. "Everything all right?" she asked.

"I was going to ask you the same thing."

"Just tired." The corners of her mouth turned up ever so slightly. "You?"

"Emergency at work. My client's been rearrested." Anger and disappointment tangled in his gut. "This time they allegedly caught him red-handed."

"I'm sorry." Lindsey pulled herself to her feet and crossed to where he stood.

"Yeah." He let out a disbelieving chuckle. "I thought this kid had a chance. I really did." He scrubbed a hand across his face, then stared at Lindsey. "I want to get deadbolts on all these doors today, and that tap on your phone. Okay?"

She nodded and drew in a deep breath.

The phone at Matt's waist vibrated again. This time he let it ring. "I don't want to leave you alone, but I've got to go."

Lindsey ran her hands through her hair. "It's okay. I need to go into the office for a few hours anyway. Plus Jimmy's here. Something tells me he'd protect me if he had to."

As Matt walked out to his SUV and glanced over at

Freeman painstakingly weeding Lindsey's garden, he realized she was probably right.

But he didn't like the thought of leaving her, just the same.

THE AVENGER STUDIED THE contents of Camille's wallet, moving each item slowly from one side of the desk to the other. Which piece should be given to Lindsey next? That was the question.

Maybe she hadn't yet found the photograph. That would be disappointing. The Avenger had thought the woman's investigative skills were sharper than that.

The Avenger fingered a business card and ran a finger across the embossed name and phone number. This would turn some heads.

The Avenger flipped the card over, frowning at the hand-written note on the back. If Lindsey got a hold of this, it would answer her questions about her mother's fidelity—or lack thereof.

It would also make solving the puzzle a bit too easy, and the Avenger was enjoying watching the woman struggle with the emerging truth.

The Avenger piled the contents of the wallet into a tidy stack then tucked the collection away into a corner of a desk drawer.

Camille Tarlington hadn't struggled enough, hadn't been remorseful enough. Maybe the daughter would be if the Avenger played the cards right—so to speak.

Soon. Very soon.

Chapter Ten

Lindsey squinted against the bright spring sun as she hurried across the parking lot toward her office. The moment she pulled the door open, she stepped into a scene of utter bedlam.

Patty scampered toward the conference room, laden down with an armload of files. Regina and Tally huddled in Tally's office, heads tipped together, voices dropped low.

Lindsey crossed quickly to where her partners stood, taking note of a dark-haired man sitting in the conference room, stacks of files and papers spread before him on the large table.

"What in the hell is going on?" she demanded, anger simmering in her gut. "Who is that?" She jerked a thumb out toward the hall.

"IRS." Regina's brows arched. "Criminal investigator. Seems someone's reported us for tax evasion."

"What?" Angry heat flared in Lindsey's face. "Why didn't you call me?"

"We figured your plate was already full," Tally answered.

Shame flickered through Lindsey. She'd been anything but attentive to the firm since she'd become engrossed in her mother's investigation. She needed to refocus before she messed up the thing in her life of which she was the most proud.

"I'm here now."

Tally and Regina shot each other a look Lindsey couldn't quite read, then met her glare.

"Fair enough," Regina said. "Any thoughts on who might have done this?"

Dread pooled in Lindsey's belly. "I've gotten two threatening calls."

Tally's eyes grew wide. "From who?"

Lindsey shook her head. "Distorted voice. Disposable cell phones. We haven't been able to trace anything."

"Threatening how?" Regina asked.

"Telling me to leave it alone." Lindsey took in a deep breath, trying to take the edge off her anger. "I figure it has to do with my mother's case."

"You think this person would come after Polaris?" Tally fisted her hands on her hips.

"Why not?" Regina answered. "If the person knows anything at all about Lindsey, they know how fiercely protective she is of this firm."

"And proud," Lindsey added. "I'm not about to let someone smear our good reputation by launching a bogus IRS investigation."

She moved toward the door, intent on confronting the investigator. "What's his name?"

"Mark Cohen."

"Okay." Lindsey pasted on the most charming smile she could manage. "Let's see what information we can get out of Mr. Cohen."

She stopped short of entering the conference room to study the man. His sable hair had been trimmed so close she imagined his only regimen each morning involved a quick towel-dry. The man's tanned skin suggested he'd just finished an investigation of questionable offshore accounts. Nice work, if you could get it.

He wore a no-nonsense khaki suit, and his conservative burgundy tie sat snuggly against the collar of his white shirt. Apparently there was no rolling up sleeves or loosening ties for this guy.

Didn't matter. Lindsey had dealt with all types since they'd launched Polaris. An uptight suit from the IRS didn't intimidate her in the least.

"Are you going to come in, or were you going to stand there and stare?" He lifted his gaze to hers, his dark eyes flat and emotionless.

Now she was getting annoyed. She stepped toward him, extending her hand in greeting. "Lindsey Tarlington. I'm a partner here."

He gave her hand a quick pump without rising from his seat. "So I've heard. Mark Cohen." He pulled a badge from his jacket and slid it across the table toward her. "Criminal Investigation. Internal Revenue Service."

Lindsey scrutinized the shield, looking for any sign

it might have been faked. To her disappointment, it appeared genuine—from the eagle's wings to Mr. Cohen's engraved badge number at the bottom.

"I don't suppose you can tell me who filed this ludicrous claim?"

He dropped his gaze back to the ledger he was studying, as if hoping to dismiss her. "A defensive attitude doesn't help, Ms. Tarlington."

Her annoyance was quickly morphing into anger. "I can assure you the Polaris Agency keeps impeccable records, Mr. Cohen. I've got absolutely no reason to be defensive."

A quick nod was his only reply.

"May I assume your silence means you won't be telling me who reported us?"

"You may."

"Very well then." Lindsey paused as she turned for the door. "Please let us know if you need anything. I can assure you our staff will be one hundred percent cooperative."

Regina and Tally stood waiting for her back in Tally's office.

"Nothing," Lindsey said as she neared.

Regina tipped her head back. "I can't believe this. Mr. Chase is due here this afternoon. What am I supposed to say? 'I'm sorry we can't use the conference room, the IRS is rifling through our files in there?'"

Chase was their biggest case, and the one Lindsey had almost blown by missing the intake appointment. Willard Chase headed up the largest cable corporation on the East Coast and was nearing retirement. He'd hired Polaris to locate a lost heir. An illegitimate daughter he'd never known.

"Can you switch your meeting to his office?" Lindsey asked.

"I'll try." Regina shook her head. "He's keeping this entire matter very confidential, as you can imagine."

"Maybe there's a neutral spot where you can meet." Lindsey plucked her briefcase from the floor where she'd dropped it upon her arrival. "Keep me posted." She pivoted toward the front door. "I'm headed over to city hall. Much as I hate favors, maybe my uncle can pull some strings to find out who's behind this."

On her way across town, she dialed Matt's cell but got transferred immediately into voice mail. Lindsey glanced down at her watch, realizing he must still be with his client.

She'd hated the disappointment in his eyes this morning when he'd told her about the boy's arrest. A public defender's job was one Lindsey wasn't sure she could handle, yet Matt seemed boldly determined to make sure every one of his defendants received just treatment.

She had to admit his devotion to his clients spoke volumes about his character.

What were the odds a murderer's son would turn out to be such an upstanding citizen? Or did the public defender role actually fit the profile perfectly—the son trying to right the wrongs of the past?

She shoved the doubt back into the recesses of her

brain and waited for his outgoing message to end. She left a quick message regarding the IRS claim, then disconnected as she negotiated the turn into the city hall parking lot.

Frustration edged through her when she arrived in her uncle's office. He was nowhere in sight.

"He'll be in meetings all day, honey," Margaret said. "Budget time."

"Damn," Lindsey mumbled under her breath.

"Anything I can tell him for you?"

Lindsey shook her head. She didn't think it wise to make either the IRS investigation or the photo she'd found public information, even though she knew Margaret was as trustworthy as they came.

"It's got to be a tough day for you, honey. You've been on my mind."

Lindsey started to ask why, but then realized what the woman meant.

April sixth.

The anniversary of her mother's disappearance.

How could she have forgotten? Shame spiraled outward from the sudden knot in her stomach.

"Thanks." Lindsey met the older woman's concerned gaze and faked a smile. "I appreciate your thoughts."

Margaret's expression grew serious. "Did you ever know my mother died when I was in high school?"

"No." Lindsey shook her head, feeling a pang of sympathy. "I'm sorry."

"Drunk driver." Margaret stared at Lindsey wordlessly, as if deep in thought. "Sometimes justice is never served."

She rose from behind her desk and walked to a file cabinet on the far side of her office.

"There's something here you might like to have. Your uncle couldn't bear to use it after your mother vanished, but I kept it."

Margaret slid open the bottom drawer and reached into the back, pulling out a long, slender black box.

"Your mother gave this to your uncle as a gift while he was in the D.A.'s office. I always thought he'd be sorry if I actually threw it out, so I made sure it came with us when he was elected mayor."

She turned to Lindsey and held out the box, lifting her focus to Lindsey. "That's what he'd wanted, for me to throw it out." She shook her head. "I just couldn't bring myself to do it."

She smiled warmly and tipped her chin toward the object. "Take it. You know, your mother had a kind heart. She'd be mighty proud of you."

Lindsey reached for the box, wrapping her fingers around the black leather case as she mulled over Margaret's words.

She'd be mighty proud of you.

She only hoped she'd find a way to live up to that sentiment by finally laying her mother to rest.

"Go ahead and open it." Margaret smiled. "I'm sure she'd like you to have it."

Lindsey cracked open the case, flipping back the lid to expose an exquisite letter opener. An engraved silver blade disappeared into the intricately faceted crystal handle.

"Injustice anywhere is a threat to justice everywhere. Martin Luther King Jr." Lindsey read the inscription thoughtfully.

"Isn't that lovely?" Margaret beamed. "I remember how proud he was of that letter opener. Those two had a special bond, you know."

Lindsey frowned. No. She hadn't known. Maybe she'd just been too young to realize.

"I just couldn't believe he'd want to throw it out." Margaret clucked her tongue. "Grief affects everybody differently, though."

Lindsey nodded, unable to take her eyes off the engraved words. "How soon after my mother's disappearance did he get rid of it?"

Margaret furrowed her brow. "Immediately. Why do you ask?"

Lindsey gave a quick lift and drop of her shoulders. "You know me. Always curious."

The reality was she wanted to know why her uncle had been in such a hurry to get it out of sight. He'd never been the warm, fuzzy emotional type, and certainly he wouldn't have been that sentimental over a letter opener.

Lindsey tossed Margaret her most reassuring smile, then reached for her briefcase. "I'd better get out of your hair." She waved the black box in the air. "Thanks for this. I'll cherish it."

"Shall I have him call you?" Margaret called out after her as she stepped into the hall.

Lindsey shook her head and dropped the letter opener into her briefcase. "I'll catch up with him later."

As she headed out to her car, she couldn't shake the sensation she'd stumbled across a vital piece of information. Lindsey patted her briefcase then tucked it safely into the well behind her seat.

If only she could figure out just what this particular piece of information meant.

MATT LEFT JASON MILLER'S hearing feeling like a beaten man. His client had entered a guilty plea in return for placement at a juvenile facility where he'd be schooled and encouraged to excel. Maybe with a little discipline and a shot at continued education, he'd have a chance at a decent future.

Heaviness tugged at Matt's insides as he flashed on the memory of how heartbroken Mr. and Mrs. Miller had looked. Just last night they'd been happy and proud—celebrating Jason's acquittal. Today they'd been defeated.

Jason had sneaked out in the middle of the night and had done exactly what he'd avoided for the first fifteen years of his life. He'd broken the law. He'd caved to peer pressure. Gang pressure. The term didn't matter. The outcome did.

Jason Miller was headed to jail.

Matt hesitated outside the precinct doors and inhaled slowly through his nose, holding the air for several seconds to clear his mind and calm himself.

He'd headed straight here from the courthouse, determined to pursue the one break he and Lindsey had gotten in her mother's case. The missing ornament.

Unless Camille had given the ornament to her coworker, Lorraine, the very day she'd been killed, there was no other explanation for why it had been on the mirror when her mother dropped Lindsey at school and missing in the crime scene photos taken later that day.

Check that. There was an explanation. Someone had taken it, but who? The real murderer?

Just for argument's sake, he considered the possibilities. If his father had been the real killer, the ornament might have served as a souvenir. Yet it hadn't been found with the bloody shears or anywhere else in his father's possessions.

Lindsey didn't believe her mother had given the ornament to Lorraine. So how had the woman come to possess it? Had she killed Camille and framed Tony? There seemed to be no motive, but then again, he hadn't pursued that angle. Yet.

And what about the supposed suicide note Doug Tarlington had left behind four years later?

Matt's thoughts raced inside his brain, crashing headlong, one into the other. As soon as he got to Lindsey's, they needed to break down all of the possibilities and work through them one by one.

There was one stop he had to make first, though. He pulled open the precinct door and stepped inside.

Detective John Parker had been the lead detective on Camille Tarlington's case. Matt had spoken to him previously, but Parker had never offered any information Matt hadn't already found in the case file.

Matt had heard Parker was up for retirement, and he'd planned to pay him one last visit closer to the actual date. But now that he and Lindsey had noted the missing ornament in the photos, he had the perfect excuse to make his next visit a bit sooner—like now.

Matt was familiar enough with the station and everyone who worked there to make himself at home, winding his way through the maze of desks until he came to Parker's.

The older man sat working on a crossword puzzle.

"Starting your retirement early?" Matt ribbed.

Parker folded the paper, turning the puzzle page inward. He looked up at Matt, visibly wincing at the moment of recognition. "You again?"

Matt dropped into the chair next to Parker's desk. "One last visit for old time's sake."

Parker's brow furrowed. "Heard somebody left the daughter a photocopy."

"And a ring. And a photo," Matt added.

Parker's eyes widened. "Hadn't heard that part."

"Most people haven't." Matt shook his head, hoping the detective might reciprocate with some new information of his own.

"Always bothered me we didn't find any personal effects for the poor family." He glared at Matt. "Wonder what your dad did with them?"

Matt bit down on the inside of his mouth, knowing better than to respond. Parker, like everyone else who'd been involved in the investigation, never wavered from the company line. Tony Alessandro had died a guilty man.

Matt had every intention of proving them wrong.

"The way I see it," Matt chose his words carefully, "whoever lifted them from the scene is just now revealing them." He shrugged. "Maybe the real killer suddenly wants the credit for some reason. Who knows?"

Parker squinted at him, measuring his expression. The detective leaned close before he spoke again. "To be honest with you, one thing about that crime scene never sat right with me."

"You didn't put that in your notes." Matt's pulse quickened.

"How would you know?" The man's lips pressed into a tight, flat line.

"Hearsay."

Parker frowned. "I'll bet." He dropped his voice low. "Listen, maybe I'm getting old and soft, or maybe I'm just getting tired of your visits, you know?"

Matt nodded, patiently waiting for whatever it was Parker was about to share. He didn't dare speak for fear he'd say something to make the man change his mind.

The detective rubbed his clean-shaven chin. "The car was too neat." He held up one hand. "Don't get me wrong. There's no way anyone messed with the blood spatter, or the blood that had saturated the seat." He swiped his hand brusquely across his face, then waved one finger in the air. "But usually there's some clothing, hair, personal belongings. Something. But this one gave us nothing.

"The fingerprints were a mess, not even wiped down. That makes sense with a first-timer and a crime of passion, at that. All emotion and no thinking." He shrugged. "That's classic. But everything else was spotless."

He leaned closer still, his gaze intent. "Not a crumb, or paper, or food wrapper or note anywhere in that car. Spotless."

Parker rocked back against his chair. "Does that sound like any family car you've ever been in?"

Matt shook his head. "Why wasn't it questioned before?"

"It was." Parker's brows lifted toward his hairline. "But once we found the evidence at your father's shop, everyone stopped asking questions. We had our killer and the D.A.'s office wanted the case wrapped up fast."

The words sliced through Matt like a knife.

The detective held up a hand. "I know you think your old man didn't do it, but we never found anything to make us think otherwise. Trust me. If there had been any doubt at all, we'd have pursued it."

"Was there an ornament on the rearview mirror?" Matt tossed the question out quickly, while Parker was being unusually forthcoming. "An angel?"

"No." Parker shook his head again and looked at Matt as if he were stupid. "That's what I'm telling you. There was nothing of a personal nature in that car. Not a single thing."

Countless thoughts swirled through Matt's mind, and he tried to make sense of them all. "So it was too neat? That's the only way you can describe it?"

"Well…" Parker hesitated. "If I were to support your theory—and I'm not—you might be able to make a case for a third party cleaning the scene and knowing just what information to leave behind. Everything else—" he snapped his fingers "—gone."

Excitement hummed through Matt's veins. "Someone familiar with crime scenes?"

Parker nodded, his expression grim. "Exactly. Don't suppose your old man knew much about crime scenes?"

"No, sir." Matt shook his head. "He didn't."

"Well there you have it, Alessandro. A little retirement present from me to you. Something for you to think about after I leave all this behind."

THE BLACK SEDAN HAD started following Lindsey several blocks back.

At first she'd thought she was imagining things, but the more twists and turns she took on her way home, the more convinced she became she was being followed.

The car had started tailing her as soon as she'd left the city hall parking lot and had mirrored her moves ever since. Each time she'd turned a corner, the sedan had turned tightly behind her. Each time she'd come to a stop at a red light, the dark car had pulled close behind her, looming like a ever present menace in her rearview mirror.

Lindsey wiped one clammy palm on her skirt, then regripped the wheel and wiped the opposite hand.

If the driver had hoped to be discreet, he was failing miserably. But if he wanted to intimidate her, his plan was working beautifully.

Lindsey had left a second message for Matt before she'd pulled away from city hall. For a moment she considered dialing his cell again now.

Maybe he'd be somewhere nearby—somewhere close enough to intercept the car behind her. She knew she was being irrational, but her typically unflappable mind had begun to run amok.

She could call the police, but she was smart enough to know she was fast becoming Haddontowne's version of the girl who cried wolf.

This time she was on her own.

Perhaps her imagination was working overtime. Let's face it, her week hadn't been what anyone could call un-eventful. Maybe the sedan wasn't really following her. In fact, maybe she was overreacting to the entire situation.

She mentally braced herself and glanced once more at the menacing car in her mirror. A chill spread through her, starting in the pit of her stomach and spiraling out to her extremities.

Lindsey pressed on the accelerator, working to put space between her car and the sedan. She might be scared witless at this particular moment, but that didn't mean she had to show it. Tapping into the events of her week, she worked to channel the fear she was feeling into anger. Anger was empowerment and right now she needed all of the empowerment she could get.

She focused on an approaching side street and cut the wheels sharply, giving no indication of her turn until the last second. She accelerated and gave a quick glance in the rearview mirror. The black sedan ran up over one of the curbs behind her, but followed successfully.

Dread built inside her, edging aside the bravado she'd felt the moment before.

As she approached the end of the block, she scanned the street in both directions, then barreled through the red light. With any luck, she'd get pulled over by a cop for the violation.

Again she glanced in the mirror, watching as the black sedan hurtled through the light, closing fast.

Damn.

Lindsey's mouth grew dry and her heart jumped against her ribs. What in the hell had she gotten herself into?

Only a few short blocks from the turn to her street, she had to think quickly. The last thing she wanted to do was lead whoever lurked behind her to her home. As she approached her turn, she stole a quick glance in her mirror.

The black sedan had vanished.

Lindsey pulled to the side of the road, her pulse kicking crazily in her veins. She turned around in her seat, searching every inch of street behind her. Nothing.

The car was nowhere in sight.

What on earth was going on?

Had the entire incident been someone's idea of a joke?

She righted herself in her seat, made the turn and drove for home, constantly scanning the street and her mirrors for any sign of the dark car.

Gone. Her pursuer had simply vanished.

Lindsey eased her car into the drive and breathed a sigh of relief. She wasn't sure what had just happened, but knew one thing. She never wanted to experience it again.

As she walked toward the front door, she realized Jimmy was nowhere in sight. The garden, however, had already begun to show improvement.

The shrubs had been trimmed, and two flats of spring flowers sat ready to be planted. Lindsey smiled. How on earth had Jimmy managed all this with no car and limited funds?

The man might have a more than questionable past, but every instinct she possessed told her he had a heart of gold.

Lindsey climbed her front steps, exhaustion seeping through her. She still had the issue of the IRS investigator to deal with, and she hadn't decided whether or not to tell her uncle about the photograph she'd found.

Maybe this time she'd keep the information to herself. The less he knew at this point, the better. So far all she'd accomplished by involving him had been inspiring a string of lectures.

She shifted her briefcase from one hand to the other

and reached for the screen door. As she pulled it open, an object on the threshold captured her attention. A white paper bag sat leaning against the inner door, its sides bulging with its contents.

Lindsey inhaled sharply and took a backward step. The last time she'd found something in this same place, her next memory had been of waking up in the hospital bruised and sore.

She lowered her briefcase, then slowly reached for the bag, gently separating the opening with her fingertips. When she peered inside, her throat closed with emotion. A small plastic angel.

"Do you like it?"

Lindsey stumbled into the wooden door, shocked by the sound of Jimmy's voice just behind her shoulder.

She straightened and splayed one hand against her chest, willing her heart to return to a normal rhythm.

"You scared me half to death."

A look of chagrin passed over his features. "Sorry, ma'am. I just wanted to cheer you up."

Lindsey lifted the bag and plucked the ornament from inside. She cradled it gently in her palm, studying its simple design. The plastic was luminescent, as if it had been coated by some magical, glowing element.

She couldn't remember the last time someone had given her a gift. "It's lovely." She smiled up at the older man. "You did this for me?"

He shrugged, his mouth curving into a tentative grin. "I knew you were upset about your angel."

The unexpected kindness brought a lump to Lindsey's throat and she stood quietly for a second, trying to gather her thoughts. "That was very kind of you." She shook her head. "You shouldn't have, though. You need to be careful with your spending."

Jimmy's sheepish grin spread wide. "It was nothing."

"The garden looks lovely already." Lindsey pointed to the neatly trimmed lineup of shrubs. "I love the flowers you chose."

"Thank you, ma'am. It was my pleasure."

"Lindsey," she corrected him. "Call me Lindsey." She twisted her key in the lock and pushed the inner door open. "How about some iced tea or some coffee?"

"Coffee sounds good."

"Great." She stepped into the house and flipped on the overhead light. "Why don't you come in for bit?"

Jimmy's smile slipped from his face, his expression turning serious. "I wanted to place the new plantings before I called it a day."

Lindsey warmed at the man's evident desire to do a good job. "Sounds good. I'll bring you out a mug as soon as it's ready."

She set her bag down in the hall and checked the answering machine as she passed. Nothing. Cradling the ornament in the palm of one hand, she tried to decide where best to show off her gift. She settled on the kitchen window, where the angel would catch the long rays of the afternoon sun.

As she held the ornament in front of the window, testing her theory, a shadow moved behind her, reflected in the glass. Fear wrapped its icy fingers around her spine, and the small hairs at the nape of her neck bristled.

"Jimmy?" she called out tentatively.

Her only answer was the telltale creak of a floorboard in the center hall.

Chapter Eleven

In one smooth motion, Lindsey dropped the ornament into the sink and grabbed for the butcher block. Her fingertips found a wooden handle just as a figure loomed behind her.

"Jimmy!" she screamed, hoping the older man would hear her cry.

She whirled on her attacker, wielding the knife, but the masked figure's hand crashed down on her arm, sending the knife skittering across the floor.

Lindsey launched herself sideways, trying desperately to maneuver away from the man before he could knock her down. She was too slow, and her attacker too large. He backhanded her, sending her crashing to her knees.

He grabbed her from behind, hoisting her into the air like a rag doll. Lindsey kicked furiously at the kitchen table, the chairs, the cabinets—anything to make noise.

Noise.

She had to make noise as if her life depended on it.

MATT PICKED UP LINDSEY'S messages as soon as he turned his phone on after leaving Parker's office. Her news about the bogus IRS investigation made him furious. Her call about the item she'd found at Bell's office left him intrigued.

His gut told him whoever had filed the false claim with the IRS fell into the leave-it-alone camp. It made sense. If you wanted to threaten someone, you hit not just at home, but also at work, especially when that work revolved around an agency as near and dear to the owner's heart as Polaris was to Lindsey's.

He swallowed down his anger, working to concentrate on her second call instead.

Lindsey hadn't told him much other than that her uncle's assistant had handed over something Camille Tarlington had once given Bell as a gift. Apparently Bell had been in a hurry to dispose of the item after Camille disappeared. To say that particular tidbit piqued Matt's curiosity, would be an understatement of major proportion.

What was it about the item that made Bell want it out of his sight? Sure, the man might have been driven by grief, but Matt didn't think so. From what he'd seen of Frank Bell over the years, the man didn't have an emotional bone in his body.

Once he'd picked up Lindsey's messages, Matt placed a call to Lorraine Mickle, receiving the answer he knew he'd get. She insisted Camille Tarlington had given her the ornament weeks before her disappearance.

Yet Lindsey claimed the ornament had been hanging

from the rearview mirror the last time she saw her mother alive—the morning of the day her mother went missing.

One of them had a faulty memory, and Matt put his money on Mickle. No matter how rattled recent events might have left her, Lindsey was as sharp as they came. Mickle, on the other hand, might have her story down pat, but she apparently hadn't been coached about the ornament.

Lindsey Tarlington was like no one he'd ever met before. Beautiful. Determined. Smart.

As he made the turn onto Lindsey's street, Matt relaxed at the sight of her car in the drive. A small voice deep inside him told him he might like coming home every night to that same sight.

The thought was disconcerting to say the least. He'd done nothing his entire adult life but work to clear his father's name and focus on his cases. A personal life was a luxury he'd never allowed himself, but the feelings Lindsey inspired went far beyond luxury.

No. The feelings Lindsey inspired bordered on something he'd worked very hard not to think about since he'd met her, but last night he had turned the corner. Last night, he'd let his heart overtake rational thought, and he'd given in to the undeniable attraction he felt for the woman.

Matt groaned. He needed to keep his heart in check until their investigation was over. Otherwise, he was more than likely to lose focus, and losing focus only led to one thing. Foolish choices.

Matt shouted out a greeting to Jimmy as he climbed out of his SUV. The older man waved back, and Matt couldn't help but notice how much Freeman had accomplished in just one day's work.

"Looks great." He pointed to the garden.

Jimmy nodded his acknowledgment of the compliment.

"Lindsey around?" Matt asked.

"Just went in to make some coffee." Jimmy answered as he returned to his task of setting small clusters of flowers throughout the garden.

Matt jogged up the front steps but scowled when a crash sounded from inside. A sense of alarm grabbed at his gut and twisted.

Lindsey.

He burst through the door and raced down the center hall toward the kitchen, his heart seizing at the sight of Lindsey pinned against a wall, a huge man's hands gripped tightly around her throat.

Matt grabbed a kitchen chair and swung it wildly at the man's back, splintering the wood against the attacker's shoulders and head. The man released his grip on Lindsey and staggered toward Matt.

Matt swung again with what remained of the jagged wooden chair, cutting into the man's shirt and shoulder.

The huge man lunged at him, sending them both crashing backward against the sink.

"Don't move." Jimmy's voice sounded menacing, angry and close. "Or I'll drop you right here."

The attacker stiffened, and Matt realized Jimmy held some sort of weapon to the man's back, but what? The masked man raised his hands above his head, and Matt reached for the mask, yanking it up and off the attacker's face, exposing weathered features and jet-black hair.

A jagged scar through the man's right eyebrow suggested today's attack hadn't been his first.

"Who are you?" Tight anger reverberated in Matt's voice.

"I'm not that stupid," the man answered, his own voice breathless from his exertion.

"Facedown on the floor," Matt ordered. "Hands behind your head."

Jimmy pressed whatever he held more firmly against the man's back, and the attacker instantly did as Matt said, dropping to the floor and lacing his fingers behind his head.

Matt crooked a brow at Jimmy when he spotted the mystery weapon—the round, hollow handle of a garden trowel. "Brilliant," he mouthed silently to the older man, who returned a victorious grin.

Matt placed his foot squarely in the small of the attacker's back as he stole a glance at Lindsey. She sat against the wall, watching every move with wide, shocked eyes. She reached up to rub her throat, and concern flashed through Matt. "Are you all right?"

She nodded, saying nothing, all color gone from her cheeks.

"Can you make it to the phone?" he asked.

She nodded again and was gone, scampering across the kitchen toward the center hall.

Matt ground the heel of his shoe into the assailant's back. "Let's start with your name and who sent you."

"Not without a lawyer." The man's tone reflected neither remorse nor fear.

"Fair enough." If the man wanted a lawyer, they might as well get the show on the road. The sooner they got this guy talking, the sooner they'd know just who it was that was after Lindsey. "Anyone in particular you want me to call?"

"Start with Mr. Chase," the man answered. "I have friends in high places."

The thoughts racing through Matt's brain clicked into focus. "Chase? As in Willard Chase?"

"Junior," the thug corrected. "Willard Chase, Jr."

"Is that who sent you?"

The man lay silent for a moment before answering. Matt wondered if he realized he'd already said too much. "I ain't saying another thing without an attorney."

"They're on their way," Lindsey said as she reentered the kitchen, stopping at the doorway. "You both all right?" she asked Matt and Jimmy.

Matt nodded. "Does the name Willard Chase, Jr. mean anything to you?"

She frowned. "The father's a client of the firm."

"The lost heir case?"

Lindsey nodded.

Jackpot.

Matt let out a low, soft chuckle. "I think we might not need that phone tap for you, after all."

LINDSEY LET OUT A LONG sigh and leaned against Matt. He wrapped one arm protectively around her as Jimmy righted the furniture in the kitchen.

The police had cleared out, the assailant in tow. Lindsey's attacker had gained entrance to the house by popping the lock on the mudroom door. The black sedan had been found one block over, parked within easy walking distance of the home's secluded backyard.

Matt planned to head over to the station, wanting to ensure every letter of the law was followed during the intake process. He didn't want some savvy defense attorney finding a cause for appeal down the road.

"You sure you're all right?" he questioned Lindsey for what must be the tenth time, unable to shake the image of the attacker's hands around her slender throat.

"Stop worrying." She shifted close against him. "You saw them check me out. Bumps and bruises, that's all."

"At the rate things are going, you'll be black and blue from head to toe by the time we solve this thing."

He spoke the words in a teasing tone, trying to lighten the mood, but deep inside he knew he spoke the truth. Even though this assailant was in custody, and Chase, Jr., would no doubt soon follow, Lindsey's original attacker remained at large.

He'd know for sure once the men had been questioned, but Matt felt it a safe bet the phone calls and today's attack had been an intimidation ploy aimed at convincing Lindsey to drop the assignment Willard Chase had given her. According to Lindsey, Chase wanted his long-lost daughter found to keep majority hold of the family company from falling into Junior's hands.

Apparently Willard Chase, Jr., had a questionable record when it came to making decisions—both personally and professionally.

The puzzle pieces of the original crime, however, remained in play. Camille's personal items. The angel ornament. The daylight attack on Lindsey.

Somewhere out there, someone was toying with her.

As Matt held Lindsey close, he made a silent vow he'd find out exactly who that person was—before anything else could happen.

A sudden thought crossed his mind. "I'm surprised your uncle didn't show up here today."

Lindsey inhaled sharply. "We didn't exactly part on good terms last night." She pulled away from his embrace and sat up straight. "Which reminds me."

She crossed the room to where she'd left her briefcase and withdrew a slim black leather box. She returned to the sofa and placed it in Matt's lap.

"Open it," she urged.

He did as she asked, frowning as he read the inscription. "This was your uncle's?"

"A gift from my mother."

"Were they that close?" He shot her a puzzled look and she shrugged.

"I suppose so. Margaret—his executive assistant— said he asked her to throw it out the day after my mother disappeared. Apparently he couldn't bear to look at it anymore. Grief."

Matt narrowed his gaze at Lindsey.

"Exactly," she continued. "It's possible, but it doesn't fit my uncle's personality."

"He's not exactly what I'd call a sentimental kind of guy," Matt added, snapping the box shut and handing it back to Lindsey. "You think it means something?"

"I do." She nodded as she took the case from him. "I just haven't figured out what. So what've you got?"

He told her about his call to Mickle. "Her story is that your mother gave her the angel weeks before she died."

Lindsey's deep frown puckered the delicate skin of her forehead. "She's lying."

Matt nodded. "My bet is Mickle's lying about everything."

"Should we pay her another visit?" Lindsey's tone brightened expectantly.

"I'm thinking first thing tomorrow."

"I like the way you think."

Next, Matt filled Lindsey in on his visit to Detective Parker, doing his best to repeat the conversation word for word.

"So." He took her hand as he came to the final point. "He said he's always had the feeling the crime scene was too neat, as if someone removed every item not directly related to pointing the finger at my father."

Lindsey stiffened, her features falling slack. Matt pulled her more closely to him, tucking a wayward strand of hair behind her ear.

"Matt?" She turned to stare into his eyes, her pale blue gaze wide, as if he'd surprised her.

"Yeah?"

"Did I ever tell you my dad was on the force?"

LINDSEY HADN'T DONE MUCH but sit and stare since Matt had left to check on her attacker's intake process. She'd run all of the possible scenarios through her mind about what might have happened the night her mother disappeared.

If someone had staged the crime scene—or rather cleaned up the crime scene—that would mean Matt's father could very well be innocent.

Her father was the only other likely suspect, and the wording of his suicide note certainly backed that theory. More importantly, if her mother had been involved in an affair with Alessandro, her father would have had the motive not only for murder, but also for framing Matt's father.

Lindsey's heart sank. During the years following her mother's death, she'd attributed her father's emotional distance to depression and grief. What if it had been guilt and remorse that had finally driven him over the edge?

She pressed her palms to her face, trying to wrap her brain around the possibilities. What a difference a few days made.

This time last week, she'd been secure in what she'd perceived as her reality. Her mother's killer had died in jail. Her father had died in an accident. Her uncle had been the star prosecutor in her mother's case, doing the family—and all of Haddontowne—proud.

Tonight she found herself immersed in a new reality—one that involved the reappearance of her mother's personal effects, real doubt about the actual killer, and the knowledge that not only was it possible her father was to blame, but her uncle had hidden evidence to protect him.

Matt had called to say he was on his way back, so she'd sent Jimmy home a few minutes earlier. The older man had wanted to stay, but she'd insisted. The lines of fatigue etched around his eyes made it obvious the day had taken a toll on him.

Lindsey climbed the steps toward the second floor, heading toward the room that had once been her parents' bedroom. She'd converted the old guestroom into her master bedroom, and had left her parents' room basically untouched. Their personal effects had been packed away long ago, but tonight she felt drawn to the space, as if the answers to all of her unanswered questions might lurk inside the bedroom walls.

Lindsey pushed open the door to the room and stared, finding nothing but deserted space. Forgotten furniture. Empty shelves. A chill swept across her, tapping into a fresh wave of grief.

She crossed to the bed and sank onto the faded quilt, studying the room where she'd once napped with her mother, listened to her father's stories, slept between her parents on many a stormy night.

She squeezed her eyes shut and waited for the

familiar sadness to overtake her, but this time anger edged out the expected emotion. Everything she'd believed for the past seventeen years was coming apart—unraveling before her eyes.

Lindsey stood, stepping away from the bed and moving toward her mother's dresser. She opened each drawer slowly—one by one—as if expecting something to have materialized during the many years the furniture had sat untouched.

She did the same to her father's dresser, finding nothing. Then she moved to his desk, sliding open the secret drawer, now empty, its contents dumped into a cardboard box and packed away in the attic. Treasures one day. Trash the next.

Lindsey pulled the drawer out as far as the track would allow and ran her palm over the felt-lined bottom, frowning when she hit a ridge beneath the cloth. She pulled at the corner of the red felt, surprise sliding through her at how easily the fabric gave way.

She peeled the felt back, folding it toward the far end of the drawer. Her breath hitched at the sight of two tiny hinges and the distinct outline of a square cut into the bottom of the drawer.

Lindsey slipped a fingernail beneath the front edge of the square and lifted, revealing a small cutout—no more than an inch deep—holding a single envelope.

She swallowed, anticipation simmering inside her. Snagging one corner of the envelope between her fingertips, Lindsey gently lifted it from the drawer. She pulled open the flap and slid the single sheet of paper from inside.

Her throat tightened as she read the handwritten words—written in a masculine script, yet not in her father's hand. She knew that much instantly.

A love letter. A love letter to Camille.

The room gave a quick spin, and Lindsey sank to the well-worn area rug.

She remembered her father's mood the night her mother had vanished. He'd left for a while, saying he was going bowling, yet he hadn't taken his ball. She knew because she'd checked the closet and found the bag left behind untouched.

Her father had returned home a long while later. Then his pacing began. Lindsey always remembered the pacing because it had frightened her, the frantic nature of her father's movements, the cold expression on his face as if somewhere inside him an emotional door had closed.

Her mother never came home from work that night. She never came home at all.

Had her father confronted her mother? Killed her? Framed an innocent man?

Pain wrapped around Lindsey's heart, and she let the letter fall from her fingers.

Was it possible?

No. She shook her head. She wouldn't believe it. Couldn't believe it. Her father never would have killed her mother. Never.

But she'd learned in her business that humans did unthinkable things under stress. Under emotional strain. Under the influence of heartache. There was no telling what her father might have done thinking her mother had been unfaithful.

Had Uncle Frank known from the beginning? Had he railroaded an innocent man to protect his own brother-in-law?

To protect you. Aunt Priscilla's words echoed through her brain.

If Uncle Frank had destroyed the suicide note to protect Lindsey and the family name, would he have gone so far as to frame an innocent man to do the same?

After all, if a family member had killed Camille Tarlington, Frank Bell's career would have been tarnished by simple association. But if the residents of Haddontowne were led to believe an outsider had committed the crime, all the better to watch Uncle Frank's star rise when he put away the guilty man.

Thunder cracked outside and Lindsey jumped, startled by the sudden, sharp noise. Fat raindrops slapped against the bedroom windows, sounding as if someone had turned a hose on the house.

Perfect. It had been storming when the police arrived all those years ago with news her mother's bloodied car had been found, and it had been storming the night her mother's photocopied ID had shown up at the front door.

Perhaps everything was coming full circle. The murder. The mystery. The lies.

Acid churned in Lindsey's stomach, and she started for the bathroom, thinking she was about to be sick, when the front door slammed downstairs.

"Lindsey?"

Relief flooded through her at the sound of Matt's voice. "Up here. In the guest room."

She reached for the letter, lifting it gently from the floor. As Matt's steps pounded up the staircase, she understood how her family might have hidden the truth to protect their own, for in those brief seconds she longed to shred the letter. She longed to leave her father's memory untainted—unstained by the reality he might have murdered his own wife.

"Hey." Matt's figure appeared in the doorway, rain water dripping from his chestnut hair. "I left your key downstairs."

He raked one hand through his thick waves, then wiped his palm on the front of his slacks. He tipped his chin toward the piece of paper in Lindsey's hand as he moved closer. "Find something?"

Lindsey stared at him without saying a word, focusing not only on the genuine caring she saw painted across his features, but also on the blatant determination that had never left his face during the days she'd known him.

He'd never wavered in his desire to clear his father's name—his family's name. He'd never doubted his father's innocence for a moment.

She hoisted the paper in the air, waving it in his direction. "I don't think your father killed my mother." Lindsey forced the words through the emotion squeezing her throat.

Matt's features twisted as he reached for the letter. "Why?"

"I think my father did." She drew in a sharp breath. "Our parents were having an affair after all. Look."

Matt took the letter from her and stared down at the words, brow furrowed.

"I think my father found that love note from your father and confronted her. He was gone for a long while that night." Lindsey knew she was rambling now, but she didn't care. "I think he killed her, and I think my uncle helped cover it up. My dad was a cop, Matt. He would have known what to take out of the car and what to leave. Maybe Uncle Frank helped him."

Matt shook his head, his features softening. "Lindsey, this isn't my father's handwriting."

"Are you sure?"

The little color that had returned to Lindsey's face after her attack now faded. Matt dropped to his knees next to her and took her hand in his.

"It's from someone else." He shook his head. "I can't be one hundred percent sure until I compare it to his letters, but it doesn't look right."

She closed her eyes, her shoulders sagging as if his words had let all of the air out of her spirit.

He squeezed her hand. "Listen, I don't want you here tonight, and I saved every letter Dad ever wrote me. Come stay with me. We'll compare handwriting."

"But, Matt—" Lindsey's frown etched fine lines around her eyes "—if she wasn't having an affair with your dad, who could this be from?" Her features twisted in a mixture of confusion and despair.

Sympathy washed through him. He knew how firmly

Lindsey had held on to her mother's fidelity. Hell, he'd held just as firmly to his father's. He was ashamed of the fact he felt relief at seeing the handwriting.

If Camille Tarlington had been having an affair with someone else, not only had his father remained faithful to his mother, but he also hadn't had a motive for murder.

"Come on." Matt held out a hand to Lindsey as he stood. "Let's go."

Lindsey drew in a shaky breath and stared at the letter in his hand. "How could she do it? How could he do it?"

"Let's not jump to conclusions just yet. Hang in there."

But suddenly the burden had shifted from Matt's shoulders to Lindsey's. He saw it in the heaviness painted across her features, and felt it in the way the load he'd carried for the past seventeen years had begun to fade away.

Amazingly enough, though, instead of savoring the fact he was close to clearing his father's name, he could only think of one thing.

Protecting Lindsey from any additional heartache.

He helped her to her feet and pulled her into an embrace, enveloping her in his arms. Heat simmered inside him as she softened against him, not pushing him away, not fighting to keep herself tucked neatly behind her ever-present emotional walls.

"I'll keep you safe," he whispered against her hair.

And he would.

THE AVENGER BOUNCED THE keys from hand to hand, weighing the options.

Things were moving too slowly. Word had spread about Lindsey's attack, and the Avenger feared the young woman would lose focus.

If she concentrated on prosecuting today's attacker, she might forget about the clues the Avenger had so thoughtfully provided.

The Avenger frowned.

The Avenger didn't like to be ignored or forgotten.

The keys bounced again from hand to hand before the Avenger slipped them into the van's door.

Lindsey had left the Avenger no choice. This time she'd receive a reminder she'd be unable to ignore.

Chapter Twelve

The torrential rain fell in sheets against the SUV's windshield by the time Matt and Lindsey made it to the two-lane road leading out of town. When he'd first made the move to the desolate area, Matt had been thrilled to get away from the more populated areas of South Jersey. Nights like this one, however, filled him with the urge to trade in his privacy for well-lit streets and brightly painted lines.

The storm had to be one of the worst he'd seen in years. Matt took the trip slowly, navigating the road more from memory than from sight. His only clear visuals came with each brilliant flash of lightning. Fortunately, those seemed to be coming closer and closer together.

He stole a glance at Lindsey. She white-knuckled the handle of the door with one hand and the edge of her seat with the other.

"You all right?"

"Not a big fan of storms." She tugged at her seat belt

as if testing its strength, then leaned over and tapped the empty slot on his side of the center console. "You don't have your seat belt on."

Matt reached over his shoulder, pulled the strap across his chest and clicked the buckle into place. "Better?"

"Much." She sat back against her seat, resuming her death grip on the door handle.

Silence stretched between them for several long minutes before Lindsey turned slightly toward him and spoke softly. "I'm sorry for what my family did to you."

"We don't know that they did anything." He dropped his grip on the wheel long enough to squeeze her hand, wishing at that moment he could bring the truck to a stop and bundle her into his arms. Of course, he wasn't sure how she'd react, and his gut told him they needed to get to the house as quickly as possible.

"Thanks," she softly acknowledged his gesture.

As Matt returned his hand to the wheel, he flashed back on the day he'd shown up at her house with the case file—the day she'd boldly declared she didn't lie awake at night worrying about his family.

My, how far they'd come.

His raw emotions toyed with his insides, twisting hard. Lindsey had come to mean more to him than he'd ever intended. Hell, he hadn't intended for her to mean anything to him at all except for a means of accessing new information.

He remembered the feel of cradling her in his arms as they'd made love. It had been a long time since being with a woman had affected him so deeply. Who was he kidding? It had been forever.

As much as he'd tried to feel remorseful ever since she'd rolled away from him in bed, he couldn't. He stole another glance at Lindsey's strong profile and delicate features.

He wasn't sorry at all. And deep down, he was fairly sure she wasn't sorry, either. She might be scared—scared of letting him see the vulnerability lurking beneath her polished exterior—but his gut told him what they'd shared went far deeper than a weak moment.

Matt took a quick glance at the headlights glowing in his rearview mirror. The vehicle had been following for miles, but had maintained a safe distance. Now, however, the van—he was guessing by the height of the approaching lights and the dark silhouette of the vehicle—was gaining fast.

"Look at this idiot," he muttered.

Lindsey twisted in her seat, glimpsing out the back window. "Why is he going so fast?"

"Death wish?" Matt regretted the words as soon as they'd escaped him. "Sorry."

She patted his thigh, sending warmth spiraling through him. "Don't walk on eggshells around me, Matt."

A gentle smile played at the corners of his mouth. She was the only woman he'd ever met who could endure the emotional strain she was under, yet maintain her strong-willed independence.

"Yes, ma'am."

But the tender moment was lost as the headlights of the vehicle behind them moved so close to the bumper of Matt's SUV they disappeared.

Matt let loose with a string of expletives.

"What?" Lindsey's voice tensed and she grabbed again at the edge of the seat.

"This guy's way too close."

With that the SUV lurched forward, rammed from behind.

"Son of a—"

The crunch of metal and the jolt of another impact shook them again before Matt could complete his thought.

"Matt!"

Lindsey's frightened voice sliced through the sound of rain pelting against their vehicle.

Matt tightened his grip on the wheel, accelerating to get away from whoever was behind them, but there was nowhere to go. Nowhere to turn. Along this stretch of road there were no side streets, no driveways, nothing but dense foliage and clusters of evergreens.

Realization exploded inside him, sending a shot of adrenaline through his veins. The vehicle behind them rammed their bumper again, this time sending the SUV into a sideways skid.

Matt steered in the direction of the slide, regaining control before their vehicle's large wheels lost traction and they ran off the rain-slicked asphalt into the drainage ditch that paralleled the road.

"Hang on."

Matt pressed the accelerator to the floor, silently urging the SUV forward, away from their pursuer.

He failed.

The vehicle behind them swerved into the oncoming lane and gained on them effortlessly, pulling alongside. Before he could hit the brakes and drop back, the van sideswiped them, sending the SUV into an uncontrollable series of swerves.

The right front tire caught the lip of the roadway, biting into the soft earth.

"Matt." Lindsey's voice had dropped so low he could barely hear her.

"It's okay," he lied, wanting to assure her they were safe, when he knew they were anything but.

He regained control long enough to glance at the other driver, but between the absence of any lighting along the road and the violent weather, it was impossible to make out an image, let alone a face.

Their pursuer rammed them again, this time sending the SUV off the edge of the road. They tipped precariously into the drainage ditch, suspended for a split second as if they might not topple over. But then, seemingly in slow motion, yet in the blink of an eye, they crashed, rolling onto the passenger side.

Glass shattered. The sound of crunching and splintering metal filled the car, drowning out the storm outside.

The seat belt dug into Matt's chest and neck, biting into his skin as it held him in place. He shot up a silent thanks for Lindsey's insistence on him buckling the belt.

The heavy vehicle slid, the crash seeming to go on forever. Lindsey's frightened scream filled the space between them, but then stopped abruptly as they careened to a stop, the SUV flat on its side.

"Lindsey?"

No answer.

Matt fumbled for his seat belt release, struggling to free himself in order to reach her. A sense of urgency and panic tore through him. If anything had happened to her…

"Lindsey!"

Matt unlatched his belt and braced himself, using every ounce of strength in his arms and legs to keep from falling on top of the passenger seat.

She moaned softly and relief surged through him as he realized she was conscious.

"Matt?"

Her voice was flat, emotionless, as if shock had set in already. He had to move quickly.

"I'll get us out of here. Are you all right?"

"Matt," she spoke again, this time her voice barely audible. "There's so much…water."

He lowered one leg carefully, wincing as water up to his ankle saturated his shoe and jeans.

"Can you move?"

"I think so."

"Let's get you unhooked and get you out of here."

LINDSEY FOUND THE SEAT BELT release and freed herself, shifting against the broken glass and shattered door of the SUV.

She slid onto her back, staring up at Matt. Lightning flashed and the crash of thunder followed in only a split second. She shuddered, squeezing her eyes shut.

"Look at me." Matt's voice broke through her frightened trance and she lifted her gaze to his.

He took her hands in his, the warmth and sureness of his touch filling her with the calm assurance she'd be all right. He guided her first into a squatting position, then pulled her to her feet.

Water had soaked through most of her clothing and her wet hair clung to her face. She wiped it away and worked to hold herself steady on the uneven footing.

Thunder crashed outside again and she flinched.

"Here we go," Matt said.

He reached to unlock the driver's door, then pushed with all of his might. The door gave slightly, but the weight pushed back on top of him.

"Hang on."

He repositioned his footing, squatted then pushed upward. This time the door swung up and out.

Lindsey's heart pounded in her chest and she willed herself to calm down and concentrate.

Matt hoisted himself up with a grunt, landing with his waist against the open frame of the door. He planted one foot next to his hands and catapulted himself through the opening and out of sight.

He reappeared instantly, reaching into the car for her. "Come on," he urged. "With everything you've got. You can do it."

She inhaled deeply, gripped his forearms as his

fingers dug into her flesh, and pushed off the shattered metal of the passenger door. She made it to her waist and hung there as Matt quickly cupped his hands beneath her armpits and hoisted her free.

They ran together up and out of the ditch, both stopping to bend at the waist, desperately trying to catch their breath.

Rain pelted their skin as the SUV's headlights sliced eerie paths of pale light through the pouring rain.

She felt Matt's hand on her shoulder and straightened to face him.

"You okay?" Even in the dark of the night, in the midst of the raging storm, the concern painted across his face rocked Lindsey to her core.

She nodded and launched herself into his arms, sinking into his firm embrace. Matt held her close for several long moments, running one hand gently up and down her back. Warmth eased through her, edging out the cold of her rain-soaked clothes and the shock of their accident.

He wrapped his hands around her waist and pulled back to study her, his gaze narrow and intent.

"Anything hurt?"

"No." She shook her head again and forced a weak smile. "You?"

"No." He returned her smile by lowering his mouth to hers, kissing her forcefully, roughly, slipping his tongue into her mouth and tasting deeply.

Lindsey wound her fingers through his dripping wet hair and pressed her body to his, at that moment wanting nothing more than to be comforted by Matt's touch—Matt's kiss.

Surprise rippled through her when a siren sounded in the distance, growing nearer and nearer still.

Matt pulled away, leaving behind a chill where his lips had been. He gripped her hand and pulled her onto the roadway, where they stood, hand in hand, watching the flashing lights of emergency vehicles draw near, looking eerily like a series of fireworks explosions in the midst of the raging storm.

"How could they know?" she whispered.

Matt shook his head, apparently wondering the same thing. "Maybe our attacker has a conscience."

The responding officer validated the theory a few moments later.

"Got a 9-1-1 from what seemed to be a cell. They gave this location and disconnected." He tipped his head toward the wreck. "Dispatch figured it was the accident victim calling it in."

Incredulity pushed through Lindsey's system. "It was all we could do to get out of the car."

The officer rubbed his chin. "Did anyone pass by the wreck?"

Matt's disbelieving burst of laughter sounded sharply against their stark surroundings. "Only the guy who ran us off the road."

The officer's frown sent deep creases across his forehead. "Let's get those statements now while the paramedics take a look at you both."

After their statements had been taken, and they'd

both been thoroughly checked out and cleared, Matt and Lindsey sat huddled in the backseat of the officer's cruiser.

A jumble of thoughts and possibilities battled for space in Lindsey's mind. Whoever it was that had run them off the road had made the 9-1-1 call, apparently wanting them to be found. But why? So they could get help?

If that was the case, why such a vicious attack? And if someone had purposely left the clues to urge her to reopen the case, surely that same someone wouldn't wish her and Matt bodily harm. Or could there be two forces at work?

Maybe someone wanted the truth to come out, and someone else wanted it to remain a mystery. Dread tangled with the adrenaline still pulsing through her system.

The storm had passed during the time she'd sat in the ambulance, yet the night remained starless. The rain-soaked landscape swallowed up the headlights from the car as they neared Matt's house, echoing the hollow darkness and uncertainty Lindsey felt inside.

If her mother hadn't been involved with Matt's father, then who? Had Lorraine Mickle lied about the argument—or had the argument been with someone else?

She turned toward the window, leaning her forehead against the cool, slick glass.

What in the hell was going on?

At that moment, Matt reached for her, encircling her shoulders and tugging her close. She shifted toward him, letting herself relax into his touch, willing away the questions and doubts simmering inside her.

Yet a ripple of panic quickly replaced the soothing reassurance that had eased through her. Panic not from tonight's events, but from her realization that Matt's simple touch was fast becoming the most important presence in her life.

She'd let the man do far more than affect her emotions. She'd let him capture them.

Lindsey settled even closer against Matt's side, doing her best to ignore the small internal voice reminding her that if she let herself care for him, she risked losing him somewhere down the road.

Sooner or later, she'd have to decide if that was a risk she'd be willing to take.

"HE WROTE ME EVERY week from jail." The depth of the closet muffled Matt's voice as he tugged the shoebox down from the top shelf.

A longing for the man whose life had been cut too short washed through him as he ran a hand across the dusty lid. What might it have been like to have had his father alive during his high school and college years and beyond?

He shoved the question away, knowing it no longer mattered. All that mattered now was uncovering the truth about the night Camille Tarlington died. Gripping the box, he turned, crashing right into Lindsey.

"Sorry," she muttered, looking not at Matt, but rather at the box, her stare fixed and anxious.

"Come on." He tipped his head toward the bed. "We can spread them out over there."

He measured her body language as she sank onto the bed. He'd insisted they change into dry clothes before they analyzed his father's handwriting, and Lindsey now wore a pair of his sweatpants and his favorite pale gray sweatshirt, weathered and beaten through years of use.

He hesitated momentarily, drinking in the sight of her. She looked as if she belonged there, sitting on his bed, wearing his clothes. Matter of fact, Lindsey looked as if she'd been part of his life far longer than a handful of days.

Focus, Alessandro. Focus.

Matt stood at the edge of the bed, tossing aside the lid as he set the box down.

His heart caught and twisted at the sight of the letters inside. Tucked carefully away for safekeeping. The last remaining piece of his father. The last contact.

"May I?" Lindsey asked.

Matt nodded, and she reached for the top envelope, sliding a handwritten letter from inside.

Lindsey spread the letter on the bed then carefully set the soggy letter she'd found in her father's drawer beside it. If Matt hadn't tucked the envelope into an inside shirt pocket, they might have had no chance of recovering it intact from the SUV.

Anticipation spiraled inside him. "Well?"

A frown tightened Lindsey's features, creating fine lines at the corners of her mouth. "It's not the same," she said flatly. "Not even close."

She blew out a long sigh and lifted her gaze to Matt's. Moisture shimmered in her eyes, but she blinked it away. Wasn't that typical? Even at her lowest moments, she fought to keep her mask of control in place. He had to admit the trait was one of the things he admired most about her, even though he wished she'd let him past her defenses once and for all.

He leaned toward the two sheets of paper, letting his shoulder graze hers. Lindsey was right. His father's handwriting was nothing like that on the love letter Lindsey had found.

"Who then?" The despair in her soft voice tugged at Matt's insides and he dropped to his knees before her, taking both of her hands in his.

When she looked down at him, he couldn't help but notice her pale eyes had lost some of their toughness, some of their edge.

"We'll figure it out." He gave her hands a quick shake, torn between wanting to pull her into his arms and wanting to snap her protective shell back into place. "We'll start with Mickle first thing tomorrow, then we'll work from there."

A soft, bitter chuckle escaped her lips. "I wish my mother's ID had never been left in my door." She fell silent for a moment. "Before that, things were fine. I had a set of beliefs in place I'd gotten used to. Now I have to start all over."

Her words tightened Matt's gut. Her set of beliefs had centered first and foremost on his father's guilt. Would she be willing to let the false conviction stand in order to assuage her own mind?

As if her thoughts had followed the same thread, she

snapped her gaze up to meet his, regret blazing in her eyes. "I didn't mean that." She shook her head. "Your name deserves to be cleared. You. Your family. Your father." Her tone dropped low and soft on the last words, and her throat worked. "I'm so sorry."

"Hey." Matt cupped her chin in his fingers and gave her a warm smile. "You're allowed to be angry and upset. Your whole world's been turned upside down."

Lindsey blinked rapidly and shifted to look away. Matt coaxed her focus back to him, knowing she was trying to hide her emotions. Just as he suspected, tears shimmered on her lower eyelashes.

She gave an embarrassed laugh, then raised a hand to wipe away the moisture. "I make it a practice not to let people see me like this."

Matt hoisted himself to the bed, snuggling beside her and pulling her into his arms. "I'm not people."

"No—" Lindsey's warm breath brushed the skin beneath his ear "—you're not."

Her words ignited hot desire deep in Matt's gut. He struggled to shove the feeling away—shove the need away—but he couldn't. The pull Lindsey had over him was too strong to fight.

He dropped a kiss against her hair, surprise spiking his pulse when she turned to meet his lips with hers.

Lindsey shifted against him, entwining her fingers through his hair, deepening the kiss. Matt splayed his hands on her back, savoring the warmth of her body beneath the sweatshirt, pulling her to him, pressing her soft curves against his chest.

A soft moan sounded deep in her throat.

"Is this hurting you?" he murmured against her cheek as he trailed kisses along the line of her jaw and down her neck.

"No." She hooked his chin with her hand and stared into his eyes, passion and desire blatant in her expression. "This is what I need."

He straightened, forcing himself to let his rational mind take over for his heart. "You've been attacked and banged up in a car wreck. This might be—"

Lindsey pressed a finger to his lips, stopping his words midsentence. "I need you to make today go away." Her eyes pleaded with him, searching his face. "If only for a little while."

Unbridled need exploded inside him and he pressed her back against the comforter, sliding his hand up under the sweatshirt as he kissed her deeply, gently, lovingly. When he cupped the swell of her breast then stroked his thumb back and forth across her nipple, another soft moan sounded from her throat. Only this time, she arched her back, pressing her body into Matt's touch.

Wild desire pulsed through him now, driving him close to the edge of control. His heart beat wildly against his ribs and he wondered if Lindsey understood the effect she had on him.

Matt took her hand and pressed it to his chest, watching her pale eyes widen once she felt his racing heart.

"You do that to me."

A soft smile curled the corners of her lips. She turned

his hand to press it to her chest. There, beneath the sweatshirt her heart beat just as rapidly as his.

"Guess that makes us even." The smile slid from her face and her features slackened, her eyes darkened.

Lindsey reached for the buttons of the denim shirt he'd put on, unfastening them one by one, slowly, gently, methodically. The simple act was more erotic than anything Matt had ever experienced.

Once his shirt hung open, Lindsey splayed her hands on his bare chest, running them gently up to his shoulders, then drawing them lower, slowly, torturously near the waistband of the sweatpants he'd slipped into.

Her touches seared trails of heat into Matt's skin, ratcheting up his desire to toss her onto the bed and make love to her until she lay spent in his arms.

He closed his eyes, letting his head fall back, savoring the feel of Lindsey's hands on his body. When she dipped her fingers beneath the waistband of his sweats, moving her hand lower still until she brushed against his hard length, he inhaled sharply, snapping his eyes open and his attention back to Lindsey.

One of her dark brows crooked when their gazes locked and if he didn't know better, he'd say the woman was enjoying the slow torture she was providing.

With that, she slipped her hand inside his boxers and traced one delicate, mind-numbing finger up and down the length of his shaft. When she wrapped her fingers around him and continued the stroking, Matt knew he couldn't take any more. Not another second.

He captured her wrist in his hand and rolled her

onto her back. Lindsey's throaty laugh filled the room, warming his soul, as he tugged at her sweatshirt, exposing the flushed skin beneath.

She pulled herself up onto her elbows and slipped the sweatshirt over her head, her now dry hair swinging across her naked shoulders.

Matt reached out to finger a strand, caressing the satiny length between his thumb and forefinger. Like silk, if not smoother, softer.

"You're amazingly beautiful."

Lindsey's eyes widened at the words and he smiled. Smiled because tonight she'd be his, safe in his arms. Smiled because she'd finally let down the wall, this time inviting him inside.

He lowered his mouth to her neck, nibbling lightly at the delicate flesh, then feathering kisses down the length of her shoulder then back to the hollow at the base of her throat. He flicked his tongue lightly against the soft spot, then pressed a kiss to her flesh, enjoying the rapid beat of her pulse.

Matt cupped Lindsey's breasts, lowering his mouth first to one nipple then the other. He tasted and teased alternately, suckling her soft flesh and thrilling to Lindsey's response as she writhed in pleasure beneath him.

"No more," Lindsey whispered. "I want you." She was about to go insane with desire. Matt's kisses and caresses were driving her mad.

She reached for the waist of her sweatpants and wriggled out of the soft material. Matt swung his legs over the side of the bed, slipping free of his own sweats and boxers. He reached for the wallet he'd set upon the nightstand and plucked a condom from inside, tearing the package and sheathing himself in one frantic motion.

A ripple of desire played along her spine as he lowered himself gently on top of her. Even battered and bruised, her injuries fell away at the caress of Matt's bare skin against her own. She opened herself to him, bringing her knees up to his waist.

"Are you sure?" Matt's voice was barely audible above the rush of her pulse in her ears.

Lindsey nodded and arched her back, holding her breath as he slipped inside of her, filling her completely.

Matt's strokes were gentle yet firm, slow yet quick. He varied the rhythm of their lovemaking as he cupped her buttocks, pressing her body tight to his.

The first waves of impending release washed through Lindsey almost instantly and she cried out with the building sensation.

Matt reached for her, cupping her chin and pinning her with his dark stare. His features fell slack, yet his eyes remained open, burning with desire, focused solely on her.

Their gazes locked and held as he pushed her closer and closer to the edge of her climax.

Desire and need built inside her, spiraling out of control. When the first pulse of orgasm hit, Matt's gaze narrowed, growing even more intense if it were possible, but never leaving her face.

She let herself go fully, surrendering her body to the unbelievable sensations he'd brought to life inside her.

Just then, Matt shuddered, his own eyes closing for the briefest second before he refocused on her, giving one last thrust before he lowered himself to the bed, pulling her with him.

They lay together for what seemed like hours, but was no more than a few moments, eyes locked, bodies joined, relishing the feel of their sweat-slicked bodies together as one.

When Matt pulled Lindsey into his arms and murmured softly in her ear, she settled against him, letting the numbing sensation of pleasure soothe her from head to toe.

She'd bared herself to him body and soul, as she'd never bared herself to anyone. An anxious twinge teased at her belly, but she willed it away.

Just for tonight, she wanted to forget the case and her questions. She wanted to sleep in Matt's arms, safe within his embrace.

Just for tonight, she wanted to ignore the fact she'd spent the past seventeen years believing this man's father had murdered her mother.

Just for tonight.

Chapter Thirteen

Regret had soundly erased the last traces of euphoria as Lindsey stared into the bathroom mirror the next morning. What had she done? She'd broken down in front of Matt and practically begged him to make love to her. The man and the circumstances had combined to shatter the independence she'd worked so hard to maintain.

Even worse, for a few moments as Matt held her in his arms, she'd imagined what it would be like to fall asleep in his arms every night. She'd actually let herself buy into the happily ever after fairy tale.

What a fool.

She'd promised herself long ago to remain unattached, uninvolved. Her heart was safer that way. *She* was safer that way.

When she'd awakened, Matt had been fast asleep, his breathing deep and even. She'd padded naked to the laundry room downstairs, where she'd pulled their clothes from the dryer.

Now she stood, fully dressed, studying her reflection in the bathroom mirror. She was weak, that's what she was. She'd let herself rely on Matt's strength. On his help. On his companionship. She'd sought solace in his embrace.

Well, no more.

He'd mentioned last night that he'd been restoring an old Volkswagen they could use to get into town this morning.

Guessing the set of keys hanging by the back door might just be her ticket back to Haddontowne, she plucked them from their peg then quietly pulled the door shut and made her way down the wooden steps toward the detached garage.

The morning sky was crisp and clear, bright blue with not a cloud in sight, as if the air had been cleansed by the violent storm the night before. The image of the SUV crashing into the ditch played across her mind's eye for what must have been the hundredth time. The grinding of metal on metal as the van sideswiped them. The shattering of glass as they hit the mud and water. Lindsey shoved it away. Again.

She paused for a moment to study the garage. The ancient wooden door sat closed, but the handle gave when Lindsey turned it. Carefully and as silently as she could, she eased the heavy door up along its tracks. Toward the top of the rails she found she couldn't hold on any longer and the door slid open with a loud creak, coming to rest with a resounding thunk.

Lindsey flinched.

She could only hope Matt was a *very* sound sleeper.

Her gaze dropped to the dark green VW Bug backed into the garage. She stood still for a second, contemplating what she was about to do.

Would Matt forgive her for running out without saying a word? Would he forgive her for leaving him stranded? And would he forgive her for questioning Lorraine Mickle without him.

Lindsey gave a quick shrug to no one. She wasn't about to wait around to find out.

She pulled open the driver's door and dropped onto the worn seat, her focus falling immediately to the gearshift. A manual transmission—one thing she'd never operated in her life.

She let loose with a string of expletives and slapped the steering wheel.

Lindsey blew out a determined breath then straightened in her seat. There was no time like the present to learn a new trick. She twisted the key in the ignition and swore as the car bucked like a bronco, sputtering then stalling out.

Damn.

Maybe this wouldn't be so simple after all.

She remembered hearing someone talk about depressing the clutch when shifting, so she did so before she turned the ignition again. This time the engine purred to life. Now all she had to do was figure out how to drive the blasted thing.

She studied the worn diagram on the gearshift then shoved the stick forward and to the left, into what appeared to be First. Nothing happened, so she eased her foot from the clutch, only to send the car bucking toward the opening of the door before it stalled again.

At this rate, she'd be able to walk back into town faster than she'd be able to drive there.

MATT WOULD KNOW THE sound of his garage door rattling along its tracks anywhere. He snapped his eyes open, reaching for Lindsey's side of the bed.

Empty.

Thunk.

He shoved a hand through his hair as his feet hit the floor. If she'd found the keys, she'd be out of his drive and onto the street before he'd be able to so much as scramble into his clothes.

Matt plucked a pair of jeans from a stack of folded laundry, fastening the button as he pushed aside the bedroom drapes. Just as he'd suspected. The garage door sat wide open, yet he could still see the front end of the VW inside.

Good.

Ms. Tarlington hadn't made her getaway just yet.

With that, the car hopped forward then came to an abrupt stop. A chuckle slid between his lips. Apparently, he'd finally found something Lindsey hadn't mastered—driving stick shift.

Matt pulled a navy T-shirt over his head and slipped his feet into a pair of loafers.

Why on earth had she sneaked out? Good grief, the woman ran hot and cold. He mentally berated himself.

What did he expect? She'd been through nothing but emotional and physical upheaval during the past week. Perhaps he'd rushed their lovemaking. Perhaps he'd taken advantage of her vulnerability last night just as he'd done the night before.

He pursed his lips as he shrugged into his favorite sport coat and tucked the love letter into his pocket. Then he took the stairs two at a time hoping to reach Lindsey before she managed to get the car out onto the street.

He rethought their situation as he headed for the back door, shaking his head.

He hadn't taken advantage of Lindsey at all. If anything, she'd been the aggressor. If he wanted to keep her in his life, he'd have to remain steady, solid, dependable. Sooner or later, she'd realize he was sincere in his intentions. Sooner or later, she'd come around.

His gut tightened.

At least he hoped so.

He gave himself a mental slap. He'd done exactly what he'd sworn he wouldn't do. He'd begun to fall for Lindsey.

She spotted him the second he rounded the corner of the garage door opening.

"You're up early." He cocked one brow, knowing she knew exactly what he was thinking.

A guilty smile played at the corner of her mouth, pulling her features into a crooked grin. "Would you believe I was going for donuts?"

"Out," he said sharply as he yanked open the driver's door.

The grin slipped from Lindsey's face as she scampered out and rounded the front of the car, headed toward the passenger side. "I wasn't going to—"

"Save it." Matt held up a hand as he slammed the driver's door. He waited for Lindsey to fasten her seat belt, then shifted the car into first gear. "You were running scared, admit it."

"I was not." Patches of bright red fired in her cheeks, and she wrapped her arms around her waist. "I didn't want to wait to question Lorraine Mickle, and I didn't want to disturb you."

He depressed the clutch and the brake, popping the car out of gear and bringing it to an abrupt stop. When he glanced in her direction, a mix of surprise and expectation played across Lindsey's expression.

"Take it for what it's worth, but I'm not out to hurt you. I'm out to help you."

With that, he pushed the gearshift back into First and accelerated out onto the road. Neither of them spoke another word until Lorraine Mickle ushered them inside her tidy home.

"To what do I owe this surprise?"

Today Mickle wore a crisp pair of jeans topped off with a pale yellow linen shirt. While she worked to keep her expression one which reflected calm, it was evident by the way she twisted her hands together she was anything but.

Maybe this time they'd get lucky with their questioning.

"Coffee?" Mickle asked, forcing a bright note into her otherwise tight voice.

"None for me," Matt answered. "You, Ms. Tarlington?"

Lindsey shot him a glare then gave a luminous smile to Mickle. "No. Thank you. We don't want to take up much of your time."

"Come in then." Mickle ushered them into the living room and gestured to the plush velour sofa.

Matt sat first, then Lindsey reluctantly took a seat next to him. She'd prefer to put more distance between them, but their personal situation needed to be shuffled to the back burner. What mattered now were the answers Lorraine Mickle was about to give to their questions.

"I know we spoke on the phone—" Matt's voice cut through the awkward silence "—but I wanted to ask you again about that angel ornament. When exactly was it Camille gave it to you?"

He leaned forward expectantly, softening his features. Lindsey couldn't help but admire the technique. Intense, but nonthreatening.

Lorraine clasped a hand to her throat then dropped it to her lap, as if catching herself making the nervous move. "Weeks before she was murdered." She nodded her heavily hair-sprayed head. "Weeks."

"Very interesting." Matt rubbed his chin then shot a sideways glance at Lindsey. "Isn't that interesting, Ms. Tarlington?"

"Very." She knew exactly where he was going with the question, and she was only too happy to play along. "Are you quite sure, Ms. Mickle?"

The woman nodded wordlessly.

Lindsey stood and paced over to Mickle's bookcase,

then back. She tipped her head as she studied the woman's confused expression. "You see the thing is this. I saw that ornament hanging from my mother's rearview mirror the day she died."

Mickle's gaze widened, darting from Lindsey to Matt, then back again.

"Can you explain that?" Lindsey continued.

Mickle's cheeks puffed out before she spoke. "You were only a child. You must be mistaken."

Lindsey shook her head. "I think you're the one who's mistaken."

Color fired in Mickle's cheeks and Lindsey returned to her seat on the sofa.

"Here's the second thing," Matt chimed in. "You stated that Camille and my father had a lover's quarrel the night she vanished, yet there's no evidence to back up the theory they were having an affair." He gave a quick lift and drop of his shoulders. "None."

"I know what I heard."

Mickle pulled herself taller in her chair. Her voice had risen sharply, and Lindsey knew they were close to breaking her story. They had her cornered.

"Maybe you can explain this."

Matt pulled the love letter from his jacket pocket, extracted the single sheet of paper and handed it to Mickle. They sat quietly as the woman read the words, the color draining from her face.

"It must be from your father." Her voice had taken on the tone of a woman defeated, emotionless.

Lindsey frowned, wondering exactly what it had

been about the letter that had instantly erased any remaining trace of Lorraine Mickle's bravado.

Next to her, Matt was slowly shaking his head, lips pressed into a tight line.

"It's funny," he said, pointing a finger toward the letter. "That's not my father's handwriting, so Ms. Tarlington and I can't help but think her mother may have been involved with someone else."

Again Mickle shot a nervous glance from Matt to Lindsey and back. She handed the letter to Matt and stood, crossing to the door.

"You'd better go now." She yanked open the door and pointed to the bright morning outside. "It's insane to relive all of this. I refuse."

"We're fairly sure you're lying," Matt said as he and Lindsey paused at the edge of the threshold. "We're just not one hundred percent sure for who, or why, but we'll figure it out."

Mickle's expression had morphed from one of annoyance to one bordering on panic.

Lindsey stepped out into the sunlight, but Matt stayed behind, standing face-to-face with Mickle. "You might want to call a lawyer." He reached out and patted the woman's arm. "Perjury carries some mighty stiff sentences in this state."

They were partway down the center walk when Mickle's shout pierced the early morning quiet. "I was a single mother. He told me your father was guilty. I thought I was helping."

The words stopped Matt in his tracks, and excitement spiked to life inside him.

He spun on his heel to face the woman. "Who told you my father was guilty?"

She hesitated for a moment, but only a moment. "The D.A. who prosecuted the case."

The sweet taste of vindication eased through Matt's system as he waited for the name he knew Mickle would utter next. She didn't disappoint him.

"Frank Bell," the woman continued. "He told me Alessandro was guilty, but they weren't sure they had enough for a conviction. He told me I'd make Haddontowne safe for other women."

The old anger surged to life in Matt's gut, but he swallowed it down. Lindsey, however, stood next to him slack-jawed.

He knew she'd considered the possibility of her uncle's involvement, but hearing the actual words had apparently left her stunned.

"Why are you telling us this now?" Lindsey asked in a soft tone.

Mickle wiggled her fingers at Matt. "Let me see that letter again."

He closed the space between them, pulling the letter from his pocket as he walked. When he handed it to Mickle she quickly turned and disappeared into the house.

Concern squeezed at his chest. If she destroyed that letter—

"Hey wait a minute," he shouted after the woman

as he and Lindsey barged through the door back into the house.

Mickle was nowhere in sight. She appeared a split second later from the hallway, carrying not only the original letter, but a second in her hands.

She extended both toward Matt without saying a word, moisture welling in her eyes, her face pale.

"What is it?" Lindsey asked as he took both letters, holding them side by side.

The handwriting was a spot-on match.

He lifted his focus to Mickle, not needing to verbalize the obvious question.

"Frank Bell." She nodded, the bitter laugh that spilled from her lips nothing more than a hollow sound. "That love letter is from Frank Bell."

Matt saw Lindsey waver beside him and moved quickly to hook his arm through hers.

"You were involved with Mayor Bell?" he asked.

"Still am," Mickle answered. "It started not long after the trial. I was young and alone. I appreciated the attention." She gestured to her belongings. "And the money."

"There never was an argument between my father and Camille Tarlington, was there?"

"No." Mickle shook her head. "There wasn't." She lifted her gaze to Matt's, her features twisting. "I've lived a lie all of these years, haven't I?"

"Join the club," Lindsey said, her tone edged with disbelief.

Matt gripped both letters tightly in one hand as he

steered Lindsey back toward the car. He waited until they were both safely inside before he risked another long look at her.

The color had returned to her cheeks, and if he wasn't mistaken, her shock had been edged out by anger.

"How could I not have—"

"All this proves," Matt interrupted, "is that your uncle and your mother were having an affair. Nothing else."

"So my father must have found that note and killed her." Her eyes searched his face, and his heart twisted in his chest for the emotional pain he knew she felt.

"Maybe." He reached out to stroke her cheek. "Or maybe your uncle played a bigger role than just the cover-up."

Lindsey frowned.

"Think hard," Matt urged.

Suddenly her eyes popped wide and her mouth gaped open. "The letter opener."

Matt started the ignition and threw the car into gear, squealing away from the curb.

"Perhaps your uncle was trying to hide a bit more than his grief when he asked his assistant to throw it away."

Chapter Fourteen

Lindsey's heart slapped against her ribs as she pushed through the door to the mayor's office. Matt had dropped her at home and she'd promised to go nowhere but to her office while he ran the letter opener to the crime lab, but she couldn't do it. Not when she was this close to the truth.

Blow to a major artery with a sharp object.

She flashed on the image of the letter opener. The silver point had tarnished, but certainly fit the bill.

Hope and fear tangled in Lindsey's chest. If the object had been the murder weapon, they might be able to find a trace of her mother's blood somewhere on the blade, on the handle, in a seam. Something. *Anything.*

On top of Mickle's confession about the bogus lover's quarrel, if the floral shears hadn't been the murder weapon, Matt would be proved right. The entire case against his father had been fabricated.

If the letter opener showed any evidence of blood, things were about to get interesting. But if that were the case, who had used the letter opener? Her uncle? Her father?

She shook her head as she hurried across the parking lot toward the mayor's office. She was getting ahead of herself. For all she knew, the letter opener was just a letter opener—a reminder of her mother her uncle had been unable to face after her death.

It wasn't entirely implausible. But her gut disagreed, and her gut was rarely wrong.

Lindsey steeled herself as she climbed the steps toward Uncle Frank's office. If he lied when confronted, she'd know it. After all, spotting liars and uncovering the truth was her life's work, even though she'd obviously failed miserably at reading her uncle during the past seventeen years.

Margaret shook her head as Lindsey approached, and Lindsey sagged as if someone had let the air out of her lungs.

"Sorry," Margaret said with a lift and drop of her shoulders. "Not here."

"It's urgent." Lindsey approached the woman's desk and leaned her weight against the smooth mahogany surface. "I need you to pull him out of whatever meeting he's in."

Margaret's warm eyes softened. "He's not in the building, honey. Your aunt called him home. Said it was an emergency."

Lindsey's stomach tightened. "Is she worse?"

"I don't know." Margaret shook her head and gave

Lindsey a tight smile. "She called here herself, so she was well enough to do that."

Lindsey's mind raced. She'd been so caught up in the events of the past week she'd forgotten what a toll the turmoil must have taken on her aunt in her weakened state. After all, she had begged Lindsey to stop.

Aunt Pris's cancer treatment alone had worn her so far down Lindsey often wondered how she'd ever recover, but if Uncle Frank had in fact played a role in her mother's murder, it might be the death of her.

"Honey?" Margaret gave Lindsey's hand a pat. "You okay?"

Lindsey blinked her eyes back into focus, forcing a smile for Margaret's benefit. "Just been a long week."

Margaret made a tsking noise with her mouth. "You need to take a day off. That's what you need to do." She gave a dismissive wave of her hand. "You and your uncle, you're two of a kind, burning the candle at both ends."

Lindsey's stomach flip-flopped. Until last week, she'd enjoyed the comparisons people often made between her work ethic and that of her uncle, but now all that had changed. Now, she wanted no part of being anything like a man who'd tamper with evidence, frame an innocent man, or worse.

"What time did he leave?" Lindsey forced herself back on topic.

"Couldn't have been more than a half hour ago." Margaret pursed her lips. "Want me to call him? Tell him you're on your way over?"

"No," Lindsey answered—a bit too quickly and definitely too loudly. She drew in a deep breath and worked to calm herself. "I mean, thanks, but that's all right. I'd like to surprise them. They'd like that."

Margaret's eyes narrowed as if she suspected Lindsey were up to something, and Lindsey uttered her next words without thinking, as if on reflex.

"Why did you give me the letter opener?"

"I already told you." The older woman frowned, her tone defensive. "Because your mother would want you to have it."

Lindsey hesitated, questioning the wisdom of asking her next question, but her emotional need won out over caution.

"You knew about them, didn't you?"

Margaret's eyes grew wide, as if she wanted Lindsey to believe she was shocked by the question. "I'm not quite sure I understand what you mean."

"About my mother and my uncle. You knew she wasn't involved with Tony Alessandro. You knew she and my uncle were the two having the affair, didn't you?"

Margaret said nothing, her feigned surprise slipping from her face.

"That's what I thought." Lindsey turned to leave.

Margaret's voice caught her just outside the door. "He's a good man."

Lindsey leaned against the wall, steeling herself. "Good men don't destroy evidence." She spoke without turning around. "Good men don't railroad an innocent man to further their own career."

She turned then, facing Margaret head-on, lowering her voice. "Good men don't idly destroy another family's life for the sake of saving their own."

Remorse flooded through Lindsey as she ran for the parking lot, her mind racing with how different the Alessandros' lives might have been if it hadn't been for her own family's sins.

Her heart twisted in her chest. When she'd met Matt, she'd carried the grudge of seventeen years of baseless hate, but he'd won her over with his sincerity and determination.

Now, she'd be the one facing him as a descendant of the guilty party. She only hoped he'd be as forgiving as he was committed.

Talk about a role reversal.

A familiar hum buzzed through Lindsey as she pushed through the exit door and out into the bright sunshine. She'd always had an uncanny intuition for knowing when she was about to crack a case.

And suddenly, her intuition was screaming.

"WHAT KIND OF STORAGE conditions?" Roger Hansen, forensics specialist extraordinaire, looked up from the box holding the letter opener. "Airtight? Temperature controlled?"

Matt grimaced, knowing finding evidence on the possible weapon was a long shot. "In that box." He tipped his chin. "In an office drawer. Cooled in the summer. Heated in the winter."

"How long?"

"Seventeen years." Seventeen years of lies and deceit—all about to come to an end. Matt felt it in his bones.

Roger moved his head from side to side, pursing his lips. "What is it you're looking for?"

"Blood," Matt answered curtly, having no time to beat around the bush.

Roger looked up at Matt over the top of his wire-rimmed glasses. "Since when does a public defender show up with case evidence? Let alone *old* case evidence."

Matt's stomach clenched. If Roger blew this for him now, the investigation would be exposed, and he wasn't about to risk that.

"It's personal," he hesitated. "And you owe me a favor."

A grin tugged at the corner of Roger's mouth and Matt knew the other man understood exactly what he referred to—a night involving too much tequila and a case of indecent exposure.

"Touché," Roger answered. "Your dad?"

The old, familiar ache tugged at Matt's heart.

"Yeah."

He waited for Roger's response without saying another word, hoping the forensic expert would bend the rules this one time.

"How'd they make the case the first time?" Roger squinted.

Matt answered slowly, knowing Roger's interest was a good sign. "Witness testimony about an argument. Matching blood type on the suspected weapon."

"Motive and method. Too early for DNA, though."

Roger held the letter opener above his head, studying it from every angle. "You'd have to get in line. I've got three more boxes of evidence to process before I can get to this."

"How long?" Hope and impatience battled in Matt's chest, and he fought to keep his emotions in check.

"A week." Roger pursed his lips again. "Maybe more."

Matt blew out a frustrated breath. "I don't have a week."

Roger turned the letter opener thoughtfully in his gloved hand. "What makes you think there's blood on this little beauty?"

Matt's pulse quickened. He knew there was nothing Roger loved more than a challenge.

"I think it might have been the real murder weapon."

"Never tested before?" One of Hansen's brows lifted.

"Never."

Matt bit back his grin, not wanting to do anything to dissuade Roger now. Regardless, the man's curiosity was palpable.

"Blood spatter indicated stabbing, correct?"

"In the carotid," Matt added.

Both eyebrows shot up. "That's a lot of blood." He pointed to the spot where the blade had been embedded into the crystal handle. "Unless this baby's been soaked with a cleaner, my guess would be you'll find your blood right here."

He narrowed his gaze and pressed his lips into a

tight line. "Some discoloration, but nothing obvious." He shot a glance at Matt. "You looking for a DNA match?"

"Right now, I'd take knowing there's blood. Period."

Roger jumped to his feet and crossed to a cabinet. "Might be able to help you out then, my friend."

Matt's pulse beat in his ears. "How long?"

"Watch and learn."

Roger walked methodically toward the wall, a spray bottle in one hand, the letter opener in the other. He reached for the light switch and darkness engulfed the room.

"What are you—"

The sound of the spray bottle pump stopped Matt midsentence, and the sight of the letter opener's handle glowing left him speechless.

The object lit up like a candle along the seam where the silver blade met the crystal handle.

Luminol.

Matt should have guessed.

"Whew." Roger let out a long, low chuckle. "Now that's what I'd call one hell of a paper cut."

THE AVENGER FELT THE TIP of the gun. Still warm. Amazing things—guns. The Avenger had never fired one before, but all things being considered, today's job had been accomplished.

Now all that was left to do was wait.

Wait for Lindsey and her friend to put the pieces of the puzzle together. They must be getting close by now.

Surely last night's little accident had jolted their attention back to solving the case. It must have.

If it hadn't, the Avenger might be forced to take more drastic actions.

The barrel of the pistol gleamed in the afternoon sun that slid through the window, and the Avenger laughed.

After all, using the gun next time should be easier. If Ms. Tarlington needed a stronger lesson, then that's just what she'd get.

A car door slammed and the Avenger crossed to the window, peering out along the edge of the blinds. A thrill raced up the spine.

The doorbell rang.

Excitement slithered.

This was too good to be true.

Apparently the message had worked even better than the Avenger had hoped.

Lindsey Tarlington stood just outside on the front step.

LINDSEY WARMED THE MOMENT her aunt opened the door. Although quite frail in appearance, Aunt Pris's eyes were more alive than Lindsey had seen them in a long time.

"You're looking well." She leaned to press a kiss to her aunt's cheek, then stepped into the home's center hall.

Lindsey glanced into the living room then into her uncle's study. "Uncle Frank around?"

Aunt Priscilla merely shook her head.

"That's funny." Lindsey squinted. "Margaret said he'd left for home a half hour ago." She spun around to face her aunt. "His car's in the drive, Aunt Pris. Isn't he here?"

Her aunt shook her head again, this time smiling, her features turning icy, eerie. Her eyes, however, sparkled with an emotion Lindsey couldn't quite read. Excitement? Amusement?

Lindsey suddenly realized her aunt hadn't said a word.

She crossed to where the older woman stood, placing a hand on her shoulder and wincing at the sharp bone that hid beneath Aunt Pris's sweater. The older woman had become so frail. "Are you all right? Can I get you something?"

A flicker of unease sparked to life in Lindsey's chest. Her aunt had been through several minor episodes of mental illness during Lindsey's lifetime, but Lindsey had never seen her this detached. This emotionless.

"Aunt Pris?"

She waited for an answer. Waited for a response. Nothing.

Aunt Priscilla offered nothing but her chilling stare, focused on a point somewhere in front of her. On the wall. On the staircase. Lindsey wasn't sure which.

Had she done this with her investigation? Had dredging up her family's past tragedy sent her aunt spiraling into her silent world.

"I'm sorry I dug up the past about Mommy's murder, but I had to." She gave her aunt's shoulder a quick squeeze. "I'm sorry if you're upset with me, but I had no choice." She spoke the words softly, hoping to draw her aunt out of her silence. "You know how I am."

"I do."

Priscilla's words were barely a whisper, but at least Lindsey had broken through the wall of silence.

"That's what I counted on," her aunt continued.

The words sent a shudder racing up Lindsey's spine.

"What do you mean?"

Her aunt turned her head, moving her stare from the hallway to Lindsey, a tight smile pulling at the corners of her mouth.

"I've been waiting for you."

Chapter Fifteen

As Matt drove toward Lindsey's office, he mulled over the possibilities for what had actually happened the night Camille Tarlington died.

His gut told him the letter opener was the murder weapon, not the floral shears. If so, wasn't it more likely Frank Bell had been the killer than Lindsey's father? Bell had easy access to the letter opener. Anyone else would have had to swipe the weapon from Frank's office in order to use it.

The killer had to be Bell.

But why? Maybe Camille had been about to go public with their affair. At the time, Bell had been a hotshot in the D.A.'s office, working his way up the ladder. Matt's guess was the man would have done just about anything to avoid a controversy that might derail his career.

The question now was, how far would Bell be willing to go to keep the truth a secret?

Matt scrubbed a hand across his tired face and tried to concentrate. That was the piece that didn't add up.

Assuming Mayor Bell was the killer, the man certainly wouldn't have left clues encouraging Lindsey to revisit the case. If anything, he'd work to keep the past a secret, not wanting to jeopardize his precious campaign for governor.

They'd established the phone calls had been from Chase Jr., but Bell could easily have been the one who shoved Lindsey the day she spotted the ring. Could he have run them off the road as a warning? Sure. But he wouldn't have been the one responsible for leaving Camille Tarlington's personal effects for Lindsey to find.

Matt's pulse quickened, knowing he'd isolated a key point.

If Bell wanted the past to stay a secret, there had to be someone else involved—someone who wanted the truth exposed. Who? A scorned lover?

He considered Lorraine Mickle for a moment, but quickly ruled her out. She depended on Bell for financial support, plus her shocked reaction earlier that day had seemed sincere. For once, the woman hadn't been acting.

A sudden realization gripped him.

Priscilla Bell.

Sure, the woman was barely more than a recluse and she'd been in poor health, but that didn't mean she couldn't harbor a need for revenge. After all, her husband had been unfaithful with at least two women Matt knew of. Who's to say there hadn't been more?

As an aunt, she certainly had access to Lindsey's house. Hell, she'd been there the day the ornament disappeared.

Matt pulled his VW to a quick stop inside the Polaris Agency parking lot, frowning as he scanned the area for Lindsey's car. It was nowhere in sight.

Dread toyed with his gut.

She wouldn't have. Would she?

Matt climbed from the car and raced for the entrance, his breath short by the time he burst through the door, stopping inches from crashing into Patty's desk.

"Tell me she's still here."

The blonde winced, then frowned. "Sorry. Lindsey's not one to sit around once she thinks she's close to cracking a case."

"Damn it."

"She called a few minutes ago. Said her uncle had gone home for an emergency and she was headed there."

Matt didn't stay long enough to thank the woman, focused only on getting to the Bell residence as fast as he could.

He rang Lindsey's cell phone as he jumped into his car. No answer.

He had to hurry.

Who knew what danger Lindsey had just walked into.

LINDSEY DROPPED HER HAND from her aunt's shoulder and backed across the hall. "What are you talking about?"

"The clues," her aunt answered. "I've been waiting for you to follow the clues."

"I thought you were upset with me for digging into the past?"

"No." Priscilla shook her head, the line of her jaw in

sharp contrast to the hollows of her cheeks. "I only said that in front of your uncle." She leaned near. "I wanted you to follow the clues."

Lindsey's heart began a steady rapping against her ribs. "Do you know who left the clues?"

"Of course I do." Her aunt's features twisted. "Do you think I'm stupid?"

"No," Lindsey answered quickly. "Not at all."

"The license, the ring," her aunt continued. "Your uncle tried to hide that one, but I knew you'd already spotted it before he knocked you out." She clucked her tongue. "He was against the whole idea."

A multitude of thoughts whirled through Lindsey's mind then suddenly snapped into focus. Could it be?

"You left those things?" Her voice had gone tight with emotion and disbelief.

"I did." Priscilla nodded, a look of pride spreading across her face. "I thought it quite clever. After all, they'd been sitting around here for years in a drawer doing nothing."

In a drawer.

Lindsey's heart broke in that moment. Her mother's personal items had been as close as her aunt and uncle's house all of this time.

How could they have done it? How could they have kept her from the truth?

"What about Mommy's body?" She choked on the words.

Priscilla held up a finger, wagging it in the air. "First things first. Don't rush me."

Lindsey drew in a sharp breath, trying to backtrack in her mind. She needed to question her aunt slowly, methodically, working through the clues as they'd been revealed.

"What about my class picture?" Lindsey asked.

"So you did find it." A smile spread across Priscilla's face. "Your uncle never mentioned it. I thought perhaps it had fallen from the frame." She tipped her chin. "So you chose not to tell him?"

Lindsey nodded. "How did you—?"

"The key, dear." Her aunt blew out a sigh, as if she might be growing tired of explaining herself. "In and out. Quite easy, that one."

"What about the suicide note from my father?" Lindsey had to ask the question, had to know. "Do you still have it? Did you lie about destroying it?"

She waited hopefully, disappointment twisting at her insides when her aunt shook her head. "There never was a suicide note."

"But Uncle Frank said—"

"He's a liar, dear." Her aunt stepped closer, her voice flat, accepting. "It's what he does best." She gave a quick shake of her head. "Don't worry. He won't be lying anymore."

Her aunt paced a short distance, and Lindsey considered making a dash for the front door. As much as she wanted to hear the truth, a small part of her wanted to run away to hide, remaining forever in happy denial.

"Your uncle thought he could convince you to stop digging, but the Avenger knew better."

Lindsey swallowed against the knot of fear that

suddenly gripped her throat. The hairs at the nape of her neck pricked to attention.

She narrowed her gaze on her aunt. "The Avenger?"

Aunt Priscilla nodded. "The Avenger always knew you'd figure it all out. You always believed in the truth, didn't you?"

Lindsey nodded, moving toward the front door. Her aunt obviously needed help. If Lindsey could get outside, she could put some distance between them, reach her cell phone, call for assistance.

"Have you figured out the truth, dear? Do you know who killed your mother?" Her aunt's voice sounded close from behind her.

Too close.

Lindsey flinched when Aunt Pris's bony hand gripped her shoulder.

"It wasn't my father," Lindsey said quickly, working to hold her rapidly fading composure intact.

"That's right."

Lindsey turned to face her aunt, feeling relief the instant her fingers fell away from her arm.

"He was devastated," Priscilla continued. "I'll never forget the night he found out about Camille and Frank."

Sadness and fear gripped Lindsey's heart and squeezed. If only she'd listened to Matt and waited for him at her office. Then he'd be here with her. He'd get her out of this mess. Somehow.

"When did he find out?" Lindsey's voice wavered now, and she winced at the fear palpable to her own ears.

"The night he died, dear." Her aunt's tone suggested she'd expected Lindsey to know that answer, as well. She frowned as if Lindsey's question had disappointed her.

"He barged in here and confronted your uncle," she continued. "I'd never heard them argue like that. Never."

"And then he crashed on the way home?" Lindsey uttered the phrase as a question, dreading her aunt's response.

"I never thought your uncle would run him off the road like he did, but then, he never hesitated to protect his reputation. He never would have killed to protect me, but he'd do anything for that blasted career of his."

Incredulity washed through Lindsey. "He killed my father?"

"Such a shame." Her aunt clucked her tongue again. "Doug had just started to come back to life."

Lindsey flashed on the party invitations and the receipt for the bracelet her father had ordered for her birthday. They'd been so close to regaining their lives together. So close to overcoming the loss of Camille.

The memory of last night's incident played through her mind. Her uncle hadn't responded to the scene. Even Matt had questioned it. She should have read the signs earlier.

"So Uncle Frank drove us off the road last night? Why? To scare us? To *kill* us?"

The thought was unthinkable. Unbearable. But then, so was every other fact that had come to light during the past week.

Lindsey studied her aunt's face, wanting to read the other woman's expression as she gave her answer. To Lindsey's dismay, Priscilla began to laugh.

The chilling sound started deep in her chest and bubbled upward and outward, growing louder and louder. She stopped only when she was ready to speak, her amused expression remaining on her face.

"Don't underestimate me. Please. I may be small, but I still know how to drive."

A noise broke through the moment of shocked silence that followed.

A voice. A murmur.

Upstairs.

Adrenaline spiked in Lindsey's veins and she raced for the staircase, taking the steps as quickly as she could. When she located the source of the sound, she froze in horror.

Her uncle lay sprawled across the bedroom floor, a pool of blood spreading outward from his thigh.

Lindsey dropped to her knees, touching his face. "Can you hear me, Uncle Frank?"

His eyes fluttered and his lips moved, but he uttered no words.

Lindsey pulled the elegant bedspread from the bed and balled it against her uncle's leg. The flow of blood was fast and furious.

She reached for the tie that hung loosely from his collar, untying it and slipping it free in one quick motion. She anchored it around his upper thigh and tied it as tightly as she could.

Relief eased through her as the flow of blood visibly slowed.

Footfalls sounded on the staircase and dread twisted her insides. She had to move fast. She yanked the phone from the nightstand, but froze when she realized there was no dial tone.

"Cut the phone," her uncle murmured.

"Stay still." Lindsey dropped low to his side and stroked his forehead. He might be responsible for all of their heartache, but she wasn't about to let him die. "I'll get us out of this."

"Crazy," he murmured. "Hide."

But it was too late to hide.

Priscilla Bell stood in the bedroom doorway training a pistol directly on Lindsey.

"Aunt Pris. Don't." The saliva had left Lindsey's mouth and her insides spiraled out of control.

"Do you know how tiresome it is to be the laughing-stock of the town?" Her aunt's tone had become more animated, as if holding the pistol had infused her with strength.

"It was bad enough with my own sister, but he'd been with that other woman all this time." She waved the gun and Lindsey held her breath. "Did you know that?"

Lindsey nodded. "I just found out. I'm sorry."

"It's too late for sorry." Priscilla's tone had once again gone flat.

"Why now, Aunt Pris? Why now?"

Desperation filled Lindsey. There had to be a way out of this. Had to be.

"Because I want him to pay," Priscilla answered. "I want to see him fail." She hesitated, her expression growing angry and intense. "I want to watch him pay for his lies and his cheating before I die."

Lindsey took a sharp breath and her aunt smiled.

"That's right, dear. I'm terminal now. No hope." She closed her eyes for a moment then refocused on Lindsey.

"The doctor asked me to choose quality or quantity." Her lips quirked and she laughed, the sound a weak, hollow burst of breath. "For once in my life, I'm choosing quality."

Lindsey's heart beat so loudly she was sure her aunt must hear. "So Uncle Frank framed Tony Alessandro?"

Her aunt nodded, but offered no words.

"He killed my mother?" Lindsey's pulse quickened, something she hadn't thought possible.

Her uncle tried to speak, but emitted nothing more than a groan.

Aunt Priscilla scowled and shook her head. "I thought you were much smarter than this."

She took a step into the room, once again aiming the gun at Lindsey. "You're beginning to annoy me." She spoke the words evenly, emotionlessly, in a monotone voice that Lindsey had never heard her use before.

"You couldn't leave him alone, could you? You had everything I wanted. A little girl. A happy marriage. A job you loved. But you still had to take my Frank. He was mine."

Priscilla yelled the last word. "*Mine*. Why couldn't you leave him alone."

"Thinks you're Camille," her uncle whispered.

Lindsey scrambled to her feet. "It's me, Aunt Pris. Lindsey. Camille's dead."

"Of course she's dead." Priscilla waved the gun. "She deserves to be dead."

Lindsey was following the motion of the pistol when her gaze locked on the ornament. The sequined angel. Hanging from her aunt's dressing table mirror.

Priscilla followed her gaze.

"That was mine, too. I took it from your mother's car, but he gave it to that other woman." She pressed her lips into a tight, thin line. "Can you imagine? He gave it away."

Suddenly, Lindsey could envision everything. Her aunt had taken the ornament from her bedroom when she'd gone upstairs to use the bathroom. She'd left the clues to make Lindsey dig for the truth, wanting to make Uncle Frank pay for what he'd done—not for the cover up or the murder itself, but for the infidelity. For the pain and the embarrassment. For the heartache.

"But why run us off the road if you wanted us to expose the truth?"

Color flushed Aunt Priscilla's cheeks. "You weren't paying attention." She waved the gun. "Camille never paid attention."

Lindsey tried to swallow, but couldn't. Stark fear had taken over her senses as she stared at the barrel of her aunt's gun. "I'm not Camille. I'm your niece. Lindsey."

Priscilla waved the gun again, this time even more angrily. "*Lindsey*. Do you know what it was like to raise you? Do you know what it was like to be denied children of my own and then have to raise you? *Her* daughter."

She shook her head. "I'm not sorry for what I did." She nodded to Uncle Frank. "But he'll be sorry. He'll be sorry when he loses everything."

The years of lies and cover-up fell into place.

"*You* killed my mother?" Tears welled in Lindsey's eyes as she asked the question, shifting her focus back to her aunt.

Priscilla held the gun steady, pointing the weapon directly at Lindsey's face. "She left me no choice." Her eyebrows lifted.

"*You* leave me no choice."

Lindsey began a silent prayer as Priscilla shifted her finger to the trigger.

MATT SKIDDED HIS VW into Frank and Priscilla Bell's driveway, bringing it to an abrupt stop inches from the bumper of Lindsey's car.

The car stalled out as he launched himself from the driver's seat without cutting the ignition, hitting the ground running. The front door of the grand house sat slightly ajar, a sliver of light winking through the space.

Matt didn't hesitate for a second, never considered a knock, never considered pausing or slowing down or contemplating what he was about to do.

He barged through the door, knowing he had to move quickly, surely, to save Lindsey.

Panic and desperation tangled inside him. He knew with every fiber of his being she was in danger.

He could feel it.

He could taste it.

He could sense her fear.

His loafers slipped as he crossed the threshold and hit the hardwood floor of the foyer. As he gripped the railing to steady himself, he heard them.

Voices. Coming from upstairs.

"*You* killed my mother?"

The sheer terror in Lindsey's tone turned his insides liquid, but spurred him into action.

He took the stairs two at a time, moving as fast as he could toward Lindsey.

"You leave me no choice."

Priscilla Bell's voice floated in the air, a threat and a warning, as if she were taunting Matt.

Could he reach them in time? Would he?

The moment the bedroom door came into his line of sight, he read the terror in Lindsey's eyes. Read the tension in Priscilla's stance. Spotted the gun in her hand, trained on Lindsey.

He launched himself into the room, throwing his body toward Priscilla, arms outstretched, trying to block as much space between the gun and Lindsey as he could.

An explosion sounded.

A flash of white light.

Searing heat tore through his shoulder as he hit the ground, the pain blinding him for a moment.

He had to move.

Had to react.

Had to get the gun from Priscilla before she could take another shot at Lindsey.

"Matt!" Lindsey's voice sliced through his thoughts, but it was Priscilla he focused on.

Matt pulled his body into a ball and rolled, pushing off of the floor as soon as his feet made contact. He catapulted himself at Priscilla once more, this time making contact, slamming her slight figure to the ground.

The gun skittered out of her hand and across the bedroom floor.

"Lindsey," he murmured, fighting through the wall of pain that had begun to overtake his senses.

She scrambled for the gun, holding it in her shaking hands and aiming it at her aunt.

"My phone." Matt's voice had gone soft, even to his own ears. "Call for help."

Lindsey slipped the phone from his waist and traced her fingertips across his forehead lightly, tenderly, the move bolstering his resolve to survive whatever injury Priscilla's shot had inflicted.

"I'm okay," he whispered. "Flesh wound, that's all."

But as he listened to Lindsey describing their location and situation to the 9-1-1 dispatcher, he began to wonder just how deeply the bullet had lodged.

Epilogue

Just as Matt had suspected, Camille had threatened to go public with the affair—including news of her pregnancy with Bell's child. Unwilling to sacrifice his career, Bell had agreed to meet with her on the night she died to decide on a course of action, and they'd argued violently.

What Uncle Frank hadn't known was that Camille had told her sister, Priscilla, breaking her heart and her spirit. In Priscilla's eyes, Frank—who had refused to have children—had fathered a love child with her own sister...the sister who had always gotten everything she wanted.

Out of her mind with rage and hurt, Priscilla had gone to Frank's office seeking a confrontation. Instead, she'd found a notation in her husband's date book and a sparkling new letter opener, complete with a love note from Camille.

Blinded by anger, she'd surprised the two in the middle of their arguing. Her attack had been meant for her husband, but when he ducked, she'd stabbed her sister instead. Once. In the carotid. A fatal blow.

What followed were years of lies and deception, including the prosecution and conviction of an innocent man and the murder of Lindsey's father.

Not long before Lindsey's sixteenth birthday, Doug Tarlington had decided to face the demons of his wife's art studio. There, he'd discovered the love letter from Frank, recognizing the handwriting instantly. He'd put the pieces together, including the fraudulent conviction of Tony Alessandro.

He'd suspected Camille's infidelities and had gone searching for her the night she'd vanished, with no luck. Lindsey couldn't help but wonder how different the outcome might have been had her father found her mother and Uncle Frank before Priscilla had.

When Lindsey's father confronted Frank Bell with his suspicions about Frank's role in Camille's death, Bell had made sure the man never shared those same suspicions with another soul.

After that, everything had been under control until the day Priscilla intercepted a call from Lorraine Mickle. Home early from an appointment with her oncologist, she'd realized Frank's infidelities had never stopped. She'd devoted her life to a man who cared only for himself—a man who had never paid for being unfaithful.

With the time she had left to live, Priscilla had vowed to take her husband down, and take him down she did.

As she stood at her mother's graveside, safely wrapped in Matt's embrace, Lindsey realized that not only was her uncle's career over, but his life as a free man was over forever, as well.

Aunt Priscilla had succumbed to her cancer not long after the shooting, but not until she'd been fully deposed by the county prosecutor.

Lindsey fingered her mother's heirloom ring, a perfect fit on her own finger, then tightened her grip on Matt's waist. She lifted her chin to study his handsome face, and he shot her a reassuring smile then shifted the arm he held close to his chest, still sheathed in a sling.

Her aunt's shot had miraculously missed everything vital when it had passed through his shoulder. He'd been able to knock the gun from Priscilla's hand, and Lindsey had used his cell phone to call for the police and an ambulance for both Matt and her uncle.

She'd known in the moment Matt had been shot that she couldn't bear a life without him, no matter what the risk might be of losing him some day down the road. She'd take whatever time he'd give her, and she'd cherish every second.

"Can you ever forgive me?" Lindsey asked, knowing fear and hope rang blatant in her tone.

The thing was, she didn't care anymore about hiding her feelings—not from Matt. They'd been through too much together, and she knew without a doubt she loved him—loved him like she'd never love another. Her only fear now was that he'd wake one morning and want nothing to do with her or her ties to the family that had destroyed his own.

He dropped a kiss to her lips, then shook his head. "We don't get to choose our families, honey. I love you. That's all that matters."

A bubble of warmth burst somewhere deep inside her, spreading heat and security through her every muscle and bone.

Jimmy approached and gave Lindsey an awkward hug.

"You promise to keep in touch?" she asked.

The older man nodded. "Can't thank you two enough."

Together, Matt and Lindsey had tracked Jimmy's lost love to a retirement community in Arizona. Matt had arranged permission for Jimmy to leave the state, and the reunion was scheduled for the following day.

As Jimmy walked away, Matt and Lindsey stood together a little longer, waiting until the last of the mourners had paid their respects and left. Lindsey crossed to her mother's coppery casket and pressed a kiss to her fingertips, then pressed them to the cool, smooth steel.

The truth had been set free, and her mother's remains had been laid to rest. As part of his plea agreement, her uncle had led investigators to the deserted stretch along the river where he and Aunt Priscilla had tossed her mother's body away like a rag doll, burying it deep beneath the sandy soil.

Lindsey blew out a long, slow breath, overwhelmed

once again by her feelings of loss and disbelief. But as she turned back toward Matt and reached for his outstretched hand, she knew without a doubt, that at long last, the healing for both of them had finally begun.

* * * * *

Look for more books from Kathleen Long later in 2006, only from Harlequin Intrigue!

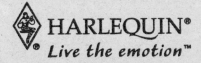

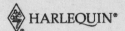
HARLEQUIN®

INTRIGUE®

COMING NEXT MONTH

#915 SECRET WEAPON SPOUSE by B.J. Daniels
Miami Confidential
Samantha Peters may be one of Miami's top wedding planners, but she's also one of the city's best undercover agents. So when a bride is kidnapped, Samantha must aid firefighter Alex Graham in his search for answers, even when it leads them to all the wrong places.

#916 RAW TALENT by Debra Webb
Colby Agency: New Recruits
Gabrielle Jordan joins the Colby Agency to exact revenge on the man who killed her father. But with A. J. Braddock, the company's best new investigator, by her side, how far will she get—and how far will he let her go?

#917 PROTECTIVE MEASURES by Dana Marton
When an attempt is made on Congresswoman Kaye Miller's life, the much younger, dashing Daniel DuCharme is assigned for her personal security. Now they each must risk life—and love—to uncover a conspiracy with international consequences.

#918 RETURN TO FALCON RIDGE by Rita Herron
Eclipse
Elsie Timmons was on the run with a secret, but that wouldn't stop the mysterious Deke Falcon from finding her. But could he do it before something horrible from Elsie's past hunted her down first?

#919 HIGH-HEELED ALIBI by Sydney Ryan
Undercover operative Mick James was set to take a long fall, but fell instead into the unsuspecting arms of Bitsey Lee. She was his only shot at proving his innocence, even though his every action threatened to take hers first.

#920 OPERATION: MIDNIGHT GUARDIAN by Linda Castillo
Sean Cutter had forty-eight hours to apprehend an escaped prisoner in the wilds of Montana. But wrongly accused, Mattie Logan didn't want to be saved. It was Sean's job to convince her otherwise.